THE SCANDALOUS CITY

MARY E. TWOMEY

MARY E. TWOMEY, LLC

THE SCANDALOUS CITY

Book Five in the Last Deadblood Series

By

Mary E. Twomey

COPYRIGHT

Copyright © 2022 Mary E. Twomey LLC
Cover Art by Emcat Designs

All rights reserved.
First Edition: January 2022

This is a work of fiction. Any resemblance of characters to actual persons, living or dead, is purely coincidental. The author holds exclusive rights to this work. Unauthorized duplication is prohibited.

This book is licensed for your personal enjoyment only. If you would like to share this book with another person, please purchase an additional copy for each reader. Thank you for respecting the hard work of this author.

For information:
http://www.maryetwomey.com

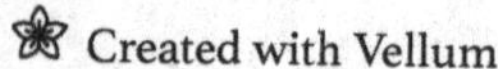 Created with Vellum

DEDICATION

For Brittney,

Who loves big, and loves well.

Leaving town seemed like the best option, but Colette soon learns that there is no escaping the horrors of Mayfield.

In the middle of Colette and Rome's much-needed break from the problems of Mayfield, things take a dark turn. Though mating between humans and vampires isn't supposed to be possible, Colette is about to learn that when it comes to Rome, even the oldest rules were made to be broken.

When danger comes for them, crashing their fragile connection, Colette knows she must get to the bottom of who is behind these attacks, or she will never be able to rest again.

"The Scandalous City" is filled with political intrigue and salacious secrets, written by USA Today bestselling fantasy romance author, Mary E. Twomey.

VALENTINO CABIN

Rome hasn't made me talk about the reason why I decided tonight was the perfect evening to run far away from the city we have fought so hard to save.

I know Rome is holding himself back from prying. My boyfriend is grateful that I took him up on the offer he made earlier this week to run away and not look back, no matter how badly the city falls to ruin in our absence.

Instead of asking me to name and define the multitude of demons on my shoulder, Rome turns on an opera I love in hopes it will quiet my silent angst. He holds my hand while the music soothes us both.

Again, it's the perfect thing to do. I'm not sure how he found out my favorite opera and had it ready to play, but at this point, I am starting to expect Rome always knows the best thing to do in any situation.

A memory dawns on me of Daddy Valentino belting out in his best vibrato a song from this very opera. I remember how weightless I was in his arm, perched happily while he gestured in sweeping movements with his free hand.

My favorite opera was a gift from Daddy Valentino, which is most likely how Rome knows it, as well.

We are the same, which is a truth I have known for quite some time.

Every now and then, Rome's thumb traces over my fingers, reminding me that I am only as alone as I would like to be, and never more than that. His presence calms me beyond any serenity I could achieve on my own.

We drive past the city until the buildings become fewer and farther between. Soon enough, we are the only people on the road for miles. The rows of towering trees on either side lead the way to a quiet peacefulness I wasn't sure existed a couple hours earlier.

Snow falls in a light dusting, giving me the illusion that we will be covered from all who seek to destroy us. The only greenery left lurks beneath pine trees that dot the side of the freeway. Even they are well hidden by the snow as it accumulates the longer we drive. They will keep our location a secret. They won't tell the world that we are gone, and Mayfield is on its own.

I could ask Rome where he is taking me, but I don't

care. I don't want to know because then I would exist somewhere. I want to exist nowhere, floating so my misery cannot pin me down. So I sit in silence for two hours, grateful for the quiet that doesn't make me stand when I can barely breathe without heartache.

The lull of the opera helps. The soprano taps into emotions I have a hard time expressing. And I certainly couldn't do so with this sort of eloquence and beauty.

The trees thicken the longer we drive, choking out capitalism with a valiant effort. I've not spent much time in the woods, other than Orlando hiding me away in his cabin not too long ago. We were never a family that went camping together. In fact, other than our recent catastrophic family dinner, the four of us don't spend much time as a group if we can help it.

Too much baggage to poke at, I guess.

We used to go on family vacations with the Valentinos, but that was before the split between our families, back when I was a child with optimism left to spare.

I expect the same non-vacation life of the Valentino family now that us Kennedys have. So when a large, rustic cabin finally comes into view, my mouth falls open.

"Is this yours?" I ask, breaking the silence for the first time.

Rome cuts his gaze to me. "It is. I bought it when my father passed. I used a human ID to purchase it."

My head whips toward him. "You have a human ID?"

Rome manages half a smile. "Of course I do. I wouldn't be able to own property outside of the West End if I didn't. And people would be able to easily track me down whenever I want to disappear." He winks at me. "Can't have that."

I point to the long two-story cabin. "Is this where you went when we..."

Rome nods, his jaw tightening. "When I was an idiot and left you because we were mid-mating and I freaked out like a child? Yes, it is. So if I ever leave again, this is where I'll be. You and Orlando are the only two people who know about this place."

I gape at the property, appreciating it anew. "You're full of surprises, Mister Valentino."

"That's why you love me, Madam Deadblood. Every now and then when things get too intense and I can't see which way I should go, I drive out here and bury it all in the woods until I understand myself a little better."

I turn my chin to marvel at him. "I love it."

Rome parks the car in the attached garage. In true Valentino fashion, even their interpretation of rustic comes with all the trappings of a life lived lavishly. There are sconces of what look like animal bone lighting the inside of the spotless garage.

I am in a daze when Rome grabs our suitcases and my purse, and then takes my hand to help me out of the car.

We did it. We got out of the city.

Rome kisses the back of my hand, looking at me through thick, black lashes. "Welcome to your new home, Mrs. Valentino."

My heart spasms inside my chest. It's a joke, clearly—him giving me his last name. Vampires can't legally marry humans. Plus, we only just got back together. Thoughts of permanence are a leap, since we don't have the best track record.

I incline my head to him. "Mister Kennedy."

If I have to give up my last name for this little joke, then so does he.

Rome barks out a laugh that surprises us both. I didn't think anything would be funny ever again, but he is always the man who challenges my worldview and takes me to the next level.

When we step inside, Rome leaves me only to turn on the breakers so the lights can show me a side of this man I never knew existed.

This is Rome's private sanctuary. It's the home he shares with no one because it is his. Every other part of him he has sacrificed for the redemption of Mayfield, but this place remains his alone.

The decor is rustic chic, because a Valentino never settles. Everything looks straight out of a catalog for someone trying to imitate a hunter's paradise.

I am grateful there aren't any animal heads hung on the walls, though that seems to be the only thing missing.

The rich polished oak baseboards run the lengths of the maroon walls in the main living area. There's a lush cream-colored rug in front of the fireplace, begging me to spread out on it and sleep for weeks. The sconces on the walls are the same polished animal bone. There is a lamp on the wooden end table with a bespoke oil lantern shape that mimics the curve of a woman's hip.

The chandelier is a gargantuan thing that demands respect. The antlers are clearly fake, but they jut out three feet across the ceiling on either side of the soft light. The buttery leather couch looks like something a king of old would lounge around on, with golden studs on the armrests.

"Rome," I whisper, still in awe that this place exists, and that somehow, I have landed myself here.

"Do you like it?"

It's not until he speaks that I catch the note of insecurity in his tone. I turn to stare up into the bright blue of his eyes. "I love it here."

His shoulders relax back into the perpetually unruffled state I have come to expect from him. Despite the late hour, his black fitted slacks aren't wrinkled and his white dress shirt with the cuffs rolled is uncreased. His thick obsidian hair is gorgeous, and perfectly in place. "I'm glad to hear it. Whenever things get too intense with work or your family, you tell me, and I'll take you here. It's a good space for clearing your mind and starting fresh."

Rome leads me through the living room and up the steps to the two bedrooms and office, which all reflect the same warm, contemporary rustic polish that the living room holds.

Of course Rome's vacation home has an office. He is exactly like me, and never learned how to properly unplug from his duty or ambition.

When we reach the first bedroom, he places my purse atop the plush comforter. The bedding is pure white, standing out like a luxury hotel selling point in the middle of the woods. The walls are wooden and unpainted, giving the feel that Rome has created a small paradise smack in the middle of nature.

We truly are hidden away.

My fingers twine through his when it finally dawns on me that my problems are literally miles away. Hours away. I don't have to confront any of it here. This place has a quiet peacefulness to it that the city has no interest in providing for me.

I angle my chin up at Rome, who is watching me process this place with a silent concern, no doubt worried that I might bolt at any second.

I can't help it that I'm a runner. I ran from my family when they treated me like an acquaintance, which is how we ended up here. Yet standing next to Rome, I have no desire to flee the scene. Rome is unruffled, even though it is the middle of the night. His trim figure doesn't slouch, though I know he must be tired. His angular jaw gives nothing away, watching me but keeping his words tucked inside.

I let go of Rome's hand and walk further into the room, my fingers feathering over the fluffy comforter.

I mean to tell him "thank you," but when my lips part, the unvarnished truth spills out, polluting the woodsy aroma in the air. "My father is dying."

I blanch at my confession, regretting bringing those words into this haven.

Rome startles, taking a step back. I guess neither of us expected I would lay it all out this easily and so soon.

Rome's nostrils flare. "What? Was he shot? We have to go back, then. I'll get Elias to a hospital." Rome is already marching for the hallway, a man on a mission.

"It's cancer, not a bullet," I call after him. "He's refusing treatment. The doctor says he'll be dead in the next few weeks. Chemo would have given him a few months, but he's not interested."

Rome turns to face me, his mouth dropped as he grips the doorjamb. Emotions I am too distressed to process myself flood his features, reminding me that I should be able to react to horrors normally, rather than finding a way to run from them.

Still, I can't feel any of it. I am mired in shock and rage.

And fear. Beneath the anger, there is a scared little girl, being confronted with the fact that her tower of a father is in fact fragile.

Of all the things the sheriff has been to me, fragile has never been one of them.

2

COMING TOGETHER

Rome closes his eyes, lowering his chin out of respect to my father's rapidly declining health. "Coletta, I'm sorry. I had no idea he was even sick."

I release a careless airy snort, as if this is all no big deal. "Neither did I."

He slowly lifts his head, eyeing my flippant remark with confusion. "What?"

Though I set about trying to explain it all to Rome, it makes little sense even to me. "The sheriff has been battling this cancer for at least two years, but no one told me until tonight. They said nothing to me. They waited until it was too late for anything to be done."

Rome's nostrils flare while malice flashes in his eyes. "I see. Now it makes sense why you wanted to run away. Good." His upper lip curls. "Let them wallow in their guilt for a while."

Rome's indignation matches my own, and for that, I love him. Just him voicing the anger that I cannot piece my way through dissipates my rage by degrees, so much that I relax my shoulders, which I didn't realize were tensed.

Though it's all the wrong reasons to fall head over heels for someone, I cannot stop myself. My feet take me to where Rome stands in the doorway, crossing the room so I can throw my arms around his neck.

"Thank you," I whisper, loving the way his heart batters against mine. "I'm so mad; I can barely see straight. I had to get out of there."

"Elias is an ass for doing that to you. And your brothers are no better. I can't believe Declan didn't say anything to you."

"Right? Declan and I talked every day while I was overseas. Every single day, yet he said nothing about the sheriff being sick."

Rome wraps his arms around my waist, hugging me like a man who knows how, though I cannot picture him holding anyone else so tenderly. He reserves his sweetness only for me. I drink from his deep well of steadiness without pause because I am a woman who is desperate for solace.

Rome holds me, his fingers threading through my brunette waves. Rome keeps his voice quiet. "So, where are we at with this? Are we sad about it yet, or are we still at the point where we want to bash someone's head in?"

I chuckle, resting my cheek to his shoulder. I'm grateful for my heels, which keep him from towering over me by too awkward a margin. "Head bashing, for sure."

"Good. I've got just the thing." He kisses my cheek, but I turn my chin so I can take what I want.

I need Rome to kiss me. I want him bruising my lips until his touch is the only thing in my universe. I want the taste of him to crowd out my rage.

Rome, it appears, is not opposed to this in the least. When Rome is worked up, it seems he does his best kissing. The tender get-to-know-you teases are gone, and in their place comes a storm of passion I am ill prepared to survive.

Rome's lips are sweet, not in the poetic way, but there's actual sugar to the taste because his breath has a hint of cinnamon to it. That's how I know he fed recently, because the sweetness is more acute. It's a cruel trap of nature's, making me crave him impossibly more.

His hands grip my sides, so I have no choice but to remain where he wants me. I love the bossy nature of him, which matches my own. But instead of taking over, as I am wont to do in such situations, my body trusts that he will take me somewhere spectacular I could not achieve on my own.

Rome walks me backward further into the room while sucking on my lower lip, not stopping until my spine hits the wall. He's not gentle; I don't want him to be. He takes my hands from around his neck and presses my wrists to the wall on either side of my head, holding me in place so he can deepen the kiss and ravage me as roughly as he likes.

Oh, how I have craved exactly this. Granted, I didn't picture a setting this perfect, but now that I am here, being ordered around by his body, there is nowhere else I would rather be.

I don't want to make decisions; I only want to feel the firmness of him. I want him to consume the darkness lurking inside of me, so I never have to endure the acute nature of this pain ever again.

I know the world doesn't trust Rome. But they don't know him like I do. They don't see how calculated his movements are when his tongue teases mine.

It's dangerous—this thing we're doing. One nick of his fang against my skin, and he could ingest enough poison from my blood to kill him. I would guess that the heat level of our explosive kiss is due to the danger factor, but I know without a doubt that even if I wasn't lethal to him, I would want this scenario to play out exactly the same.

Rome draws my wrists over my head while he bruises my lips, barely giving me room for breath. He drags them above me, pinning them to the wall over my head in one of his capable hands, so the other can trace the curve of my hip.

But his hand doesn't stop there.

Desire floods me when Rome draws a line down my thigh and then brings it back up, hiking my skirt so the scandal of my bare leg is exposed to the cabin.

My leg acts on its own, hooking itself around his thigh so my heel can pin him that much closer. The thrill of his body trapping mine to the wall is a treat I never dreamed I would enjoy this much.

I want him. I need him closer. My body heats to a level I cannot quell on my own, nor can I wait another minute for Rome to take what has been his from the first time he teased me with his knowing smile.

His hips move against mine, giving me friction that I am too tongue-tied to ask for. Rome knows me. He understands my body well enough to give it what it craves. When his trousers slip over his hips, there is no question that neither of us will be stopping the inevitable.

I writhe against him, unable to gather up any semblance of self-control. I am a woman possessed, taking the best pleasure life has to offer while my breath hitches and my eyes roll back.

Rome's fingers dip below the hem of my hiked skirt, moving aside any offending fabric that might keep us from each other. While his tongue plunders my mouth, his fingers dance on the edge of the silk I keep hidden from the world. He traces and teases like a man who knows what he's doing.

His wicked chuckle tells me he enjoys the sights and

sounds of me coming undone by a mere few swipes of his fingers.

There will be no more waiting. Finally, I take what I want, and Rome gives it to me in spades. I love the feel of our connection so much that I cry out when his hips slam against me.

Rome breathes through gritted teeth as his movements grow frenzied and forcefully decadent.

A whimper escapes my lips when an odd thing happens to my vision, interrupting the journey up the mountain I am quickly hurtling toward. Blue and silver swirls spark in my periphery, whether I have my eyes opened or closed. I don't understand it, but I am too far gone to stop and analyze.

Rome cries out, but not in pleasure. There is a fear to the sound that scares me. Rome is always in control, always planning and making his way to his next move of power.

When he opens his eyes and pulls back for a quick breath, there's a dazed look about him, like he's high on some drug that must be incredible.

Me. I am the drug that's bringing about that euphoria on his features.

He growls like a lion, the tease of the evening sufficiently gone for the night. I startle when he lunges, smashing me to the wall without finesse.

I cry out, my senses consumed with him. The glittery

swirls in my vision grow bigger, more intense as our bodies marry together without need for a barrier of propriety.

This is the way we should always be. My pelvis is magnetized to his, unable to stop, barring a natural disaster. I want to chase this sensation, this utter overwhelm that is making the blue and silver swirls pulse and finally climax around us. My face is pinched as my eyes roll back.

I need this. I need him.

Fireworks dance in my vision. I'm not sure if I am breathing, if I am even alive, or if I am floating in some blissful place in between. All I know is that this is where I will always want to be.

But Rome is not finished.

Rome's fingers dig deep into my thigh, gripping me to keep a rhythm going that neither of us can stop. He doesn't moan against my lips, but grunts, breathing through his teeth while we chase every forbidden way we could possibly set the world on fire.

We fall over the edge of the cliff within seconds of each other, shuddering together and losing hold of our kiss that was so controlled mere minutes ago.

I love the way he sounds when he is helplessly lost for me.

Rome cries out as the blue and silver swirls overtake us, tangling through our limbs and piercing parts of my soul that I thought would remain forever untouched. The glittery strings of fireworks scream in their silent way as the colors elongate and stretch, bombarding me with their brightness.

I sag against the wall, pinned in place by Rome's shuddering body as the colors burst and begin to rain down on us. Our skin and clothing are spattered with opaque paint, making us part of a scandalous portrait I didn't realize I was posing for.

The paint drips and swirls cohesively down our bodies, almost as if it is tying our essences together. I don't know how I am certain of this, but I know that now we can weather any storm that might come up against us.

A blue stroke of shimmering paint that starts on his cheek smooths onto mine, like one amalgamated brushstroke of beauty that bonds us forever together.

The world brightens without my permission, so much that either I close my eyes, or I temporarily go blind. It's for a flash of a second, but I can tell Rome sees it, too. Our gasp happens at the same time.

I am breathing hard as I come down from the euphoria, letting it remain in my body for as long as it likes.

Rome is on the decline, too, his gasps ragged as we sag against each other. He drops my wrists and stumbles back, his eyes lidded as he casts around for the nearest spot to land after such an intense connection.

I stumble on rubbery legs to the bed, flopping ungracefully atop the plush snow-colored comforter while my heart finds a more sustainable rhythm.

"What the…" Rome trails off as he slumps on the side of the bed, fumbling with his zipper. I can tell it's a great effort for him to lift his legs to rest them on the bed beside me. When his head falls to the pillow, his breathing is as uneven as mine. "What was that?"

I was hoping he could tell me. I'm way out of my depth, here. "Is this what it's like to get it on with a vampire? I've never had hallucinations before. Did you see all that?"

"The blue and silver designs?" He checks his arms for paint, but the colors have deserted us, leaving us both breathless.

I burrow atop the covers, making a nest for myself so I can be cradled while the world settles blissfully around me.

"Coletta, I…" Rome's voice is quiet, but shifts so that it is strained with anxiety. "You have to go," he finally works out.

3

THE ONLY HELP I CAN GIVE

Whatever relaxation I was hoping to get leaves me in a gust the moment Rome tells me to exit the bedroom in which we just shared an earth-splitting connection. "What?"

"Out, Coletta." Rome grips the fabric over his heart. "You can't be here!"

I startle with the strength of his volume that comes to me out of nowhere. Tears prick my eyes as I fumble atop the bed. I struggle to sit up and make sense of the world. "I don't understand. We just... Why would you tell me to leave? Why are you doing this to us again?" My heart threatens to rupture in my chest. "Things got intense last time and you left. We just... and now I have to go?"

It's only now that I am sitting up that I notice a flash of Rome's fangs while he tenses atop the bed.

They are longer than they should be.

My eyes widen when the consequences of dating a vampire begin to envelope me.

Rome grips the white down comforter while his neck muscles strain. "I need blood! Whatever that was took a lot out of me. I just fed this morning, but suddenly it's like I haven't drank in weeks. I need blood now, and if I sink my fangs into your neck, I'll die. Go, Colette! Run!"

His command takes on a mournful keening sound that tugs at my heartstrings.

"You won't hurt me," I assure him, confident in this one truth. I lean over and hold his hand, unable to leave his side after the cataclysmic experience we shared.

He tugs at his hair with his free hand. "You can't know that! I can hear your heart beating. I have to feed, and there's no blood for miles! Run, Colette!"

It's a dangerous bet I'm taking, but I roll the dice with both our lives and grip his hand tighter. With my free hand, I slide his phone from his pocket and dial his cousin.

Orlando's gruff voice does not disappoint. "I took care of the halluci-den on Vista Street. Four deaths, but still no source. I shot too fast. They weren't exactly reasonable when I went in there. They pounced, so I shot first before I could ask questions. Still no sign of Frank's kid."

I can picture Orlando stiffening when it's my voice that replies, and not Rome's. "Orlando, I need your help. We did something, Rome and me, and Rome needs blood."

A long pause fills my ears while Rome writhes on the bed. Orlando shifts his tone, now that he knows who he is talking to. "Rome fed this morning. He'll be fine for another week, at least. I appreciate you worrying about him, but Rome is a big boy. He knows how to feed himself."

I grit my teeth as Rome squeezes my fingers too tight for comfort. He snatches the phone from me, not bothering to conceal his panic as he shouts into the device. "Orlando, I need blood! All the symptoms are there. I'm on the edge of feral. I need blood now!"

Orlando's reply comes quick. "What could you possibly have done? Did you get injured?"

"No! Orlando, hurry!"

"On it, boss. I've got an emergency blood bag in my car, and I'm turning around to drive it out to you."

I grasp at any way to be helpful. "What about the flask of your blood that you gave me, Orlando?"

But before he answers, I know what he is going to say. "Vampires can't feed off each other. It's a different substance altogether. We need human blood. Vampire blood makes us think we're full, but it does nothing to help a vampire's body."

Duh. I know this. I'm not thinking straight.

Rome fists his fingers in his black hair, pulling hard. "Whatever you're bringing me, it's not soon enough! I'm telling you, I'm starved. My body is reacting like I haven't fed in a month!"

Orlando swears. "Alright. Okay, Rome. Deep breaths. Coco, can you hear me?"

Tears prick my eyes as I kneel on the bed beside the man I love while he writhes in agony. "Yes! Orlando, what do I do?"

Orlando's reply leaves no room for argument. "Get out of there! Take Rome's keys and lock yourself in his car, understood?"

"I can't leave him like this! He's in pain!"

"Is he wounded? Is he bleeding anywhere that you can tell?"

I examine Rome for the smallest papercut, noting his breathing that grows more labored by the minute. "No. What's happening?"

"You're taking his keys, Coco. That's what's happening."

Before I can protest again, Rome is already pulling his keys from his pocket and pressing them into my palm. "Go, tré-sur. Run quick. Lock yourself inside. Do not let me in, no matter what."

Tears wet the apples of my cheeks. "No! Rome, I don't understand how this happened! Did I hurt you?"

"No, little cannoli." Rome forces a smile that looks more like a grimace. "You could never hurt me."

My chest shudders as my tears fall, dotting his shirt as I lean over his supine form.

Orlando is irate on the other end. "Coco, listen to me.

You very much can hurt him. You could kill him if he loses his mind. I'm not sure how, but it sounds like he's on the edge of that as we speak. If a vampire gets too thirsty, we turn feral."

"I don't want to desert him! I care about him, Orlando."

The forbidding figure pauses, his voice softening. "I know you do. That's good. Because you care about him, you need to run to the car. On your feet, Colette my dove."

The sweet and usually funny nickname Orlando has for me snaps some sense into my brain. Of all the times I have dealt with my problems by running away, this is the one time I very much want to stay in one place while life's uncertainties crash over me. But I listen to Orlando, trusting that he loves us both enough to know the right thing to do.

Slowly, I consent to stand from the bed, but only because Rome begins to look at me as if he is afraid of my very presence. "There are bags under his eyes now," I tell Orlando. "They weren't there a minute ago. Purple in the hollows of his eyes. It's making his irises brighter. His fangs are longer."

Orlando swears. "Tell me where you are in the cabin."

"I'm in the upstairs guest bedroom."

"Wrong. You're in the car. Move your feet, little dove."

I sniffle back my emotion, but it does nothing to hide my angst. "I'm sorry, Rome!"

A feral growl emanates from him, his upper lip curling

to reveal a fang that can only be used for carnage and never kissing. "Go slowly," Rome warns. "If you run, I'll give chase. The monster in me is taking over."

Orlando's cadence is a forced calm. "Into the hallway, Coco."

"I'm doing it," I whisper, my sobs quiet yet uncontrollable. "I'll start travelling with blood bags in my car. I won't let this happen to him ever again. I promise I'll be good for him!"

Orlando's steady demeanor is the only thing tethering me to the planet. It is clear that Orlando and I are mated because I trust him enough to go where he tells me. "You already are. This isn't normal. Rome never lets himself get depleted. It's not your fault. It's a fluke. We just need everyone to get out of this alive, okay? Then we can deal with the how and why of it all. Down the steps, little dove."

My heels click on the wood, increasing the rapid thrum of my heart. It feels like I am lost in a horror movie, sneaking through the cabin while the killer is on the prowl.

Except Rome could never be a killer. He's good to me.

"I'm in the living room," I whisper, clutching the keys like I'm holding a knife that I definitely don't want to have to use.

"That's good. Open the door slowly. Leave it open. If it shuts too hard, it'll set his monster off."

"He is not a monster!" I protest, pained at the very

thought. "Rome is a gentleman. No part of him could ever be a monster!"

Despite the tension, Orlando chuckles. It's a warm, deep sound that I forgot existed. I'm sure most people would argue that Orlando isn't capable of such a sweet sound, but they don't know him like I do. "Wow. I'm glad he has you, Coco. No one loves Rome like that. Good. Keep that rose-colored version of him tight in your heart." He pauses. "I don't hear the door."

I'm careful, quiet as I twist the handle. "I'm out," I whisper, though the small sound feels like a shout loud enough to wake the dead.

Rome howls from upstairs, but I don't hear footsteps. A rabid growl tears up the night as I walk into the frosty moonlit outdoors. The haunting sound coupled with the inch of snow on the ground chills my blood in my veins.

I don't want to be scared, not of Rome. He knows which opera I like and doesn't make me talk about things until I am ready. He kisses like a dirty dream and holds my hand like a fairytale prince.

The desire to run is heavy in my bones, but I will my body never to run from Rome. He is good for me—good *to* me—which is a thing I didn't realize a person needed.

"I'm in the car," I finally tell Orlando, shutting the door as quietly as one can accomplish such a thing.

"Good, Coco. That's real good. Let me hear the locks."

I secure myself inside, and finally let loose more tears

than I realized I currently had on standby. "I can feel him even out here! He's scared, Orlando! He doesn't know why he's so hungry." A flash of Rome infiltrates my mind's eye, jerking emotion around in my ribcage. "He's biting himself!" I can see it clearly, though there is no way I possibly could. Still, I am certain of this fact. Rome is gripping the headboard, gnawing on his knuckles. He is drawing blood that doesn't sustain in hopes he can trick his brain to lay off for a few minutes so he can breathe without fire in his lungs.

Orlando is livid. "I thought you were in the car!"

"I am! But when I close my eyes, I know that's what he's doing up there in the bedroom! Rome is biting the knuckles on his left hand, sucking as much blood as he can."

"You're crazy," Orlando replies dismissively. "You're safe if you're in the car, alright? So stay there. I'm on my way. If he's as bad off as you say, then I have to stop and pick up more blood, otherwise this bag will be a drop in the bucket of what he needs."

"Hurry!" My heart aches to go to my bedraggled boyfriend. It's torture to know he is in agony. The only way I can help him is to put distance between my body and his. Still, I force myself to be separate from his pain. "Orlando, he's banging his head against the headboard!"

"What? Colette, if you can't see him, then you don't know that's true. You're getting hysterical."

Of all the things to call a woman mid-crisis, "hysterical" is the wrong choice. Steel coats my words like venom-laced bullets ready to be fired. "Orlando, I'm telling you, I can see him in my mind. Rome is trying to knock himself out. He's scared. Is there blood nearby that I can get for him?"

Orlando's pause is not reassuring. "No. Even if there was, no one would sell to you. You're not a vampire."

My bleat of defeat bleeds through my body, weighting me so much that all I can do is press my forehead to the steering wheel while visions of Rome bashing his head against the wall plague my mind.

My vision blurs when he hits himself particularly hard. My head smarts at the point of contact, though I know I didn't hit my head.

Fear pulses through me because I cannot have another head injury. I worked too hard to recover from the last one that left me in a wheelchair and completely dependent upon my nurse.

On the next blow of Rome's head to his headboard, I slump against the steering wheel, my jaw going slack. Orlando calls my name, but I can't answer.

I came to the woods with my boyfriend to run away from the chaos, but it seems the tornado of uncertainty will follow me wherever I go.

"Colette! Colette, say something!"

But the world is dimming so much that there is no

point in struggling to reply. Orlando's voice is the last thing I hear before I pass clean out.

4

THE SPACE BETWEEN US

When thick arms cradle my body, I'm certain I am dreaming, only I can't remember much that happened before this. The icy air nips at my skin, letting me know I am exposed to the wintry elements.

A male voice swears in a steady, barely coherent stream, though he sounds far away. Or perhaps I am hearing everything through a tunnel.

My head lolls over the beefy forearm. "Don't take me," I manage in a barely coherent moan. I don't want to be kidnapped again. I mean, I didn't prefer it the first three times, but I'm in no mood for it now. My head is pounding, my temples tight with an intense pressure I cannot get rid of. I can't even lift my arms to massage my temples.

Something has happened to my faculties, draining me

of my energy so much that I can't fight the man who is taking me from Rome's car and back into the cabin.

"I've got her, Rome. Calm yourself down. You'll do no one any good if you're jittery like that."

It's Orlando. The tunnel effect is clearing, though I still don't have control over my body.

"Give her to me, Orlando!" Rome growls, though the sound has a weary quality to it.

"Not until you can hold that mug without dropping it. You could crush her if you're not careful. I saw what you did to the door."

"Now!" Rome roars. He actually roars. There's a tinny quality to the sound, letting me know that whatever hallucination I am having, it hasn't passed yet.

There's a cry of desperation and then a high-pitched crash of something against the wall.

I'm guessing that was the mug.

Orlando clutches me tighter to his chest. "If you think that's you calming down, you're wrong. I don't care how hopped up on love juice you are, Coco is staying in my arms until you can hold a mug for an entire minute without breaking it."

I blink, opening my eyes to welcome the living room of the two-story cabin, though the setting is blurred while my headache tries to reason with my vision.

Orlando catches the heavy front door with his foot and swings it shut behind him.

Rome's voice is trembling with desperation. "You know I won't hurt her! She's not a mug I can shatter."

"You're right. You won't hurt her. Because you're not getting near her until I say so. She's the Last Deadblood, Rome. One wrong move, and you start a war. I'm still waiting on an explanation of how she ended up passed out in your car."

"Rome banged his head," I explain, though as I say this, I'm unsure how lucid I actually am, and therefore, I am not confident of how credible my testimony could possibly be.

Orlando stiffens, no doubt surprised that I'm awake. "Rome hitting his head in the bedroom inside the cabin has nothing to do with you passing out in the car outside."

I turn my head just in time to see Rome dropping to his knees, gripping the wood floor as intensity rocks through his body. "Coletta, I'm sorry. I don't know how that happened, how I almost... I've never been that low on blood."

I kick my legs haphazardly. "Let me down, Orlando."

Orlando coils his fingers more tightly around my body, but I can feel him caving. "Easy, Coco. He's not himself yet."

Vampires only go to full strength when they've turned rabid—deprived of blood until all they can see are pulses—nature's way of leading them to sustenance. Their bodies amp up, going into survival mode, where people aren't people, and no one has to be willing.

Their prey doesn't have to survive, either.

That's usually how those types of situations pan out.

The moment Orlando sets my feet on the floor, I make to run to Rome, but it's a bad start. My legs are rubbery, coupled with the fact that I am still wearing high heels. My knees go out from under me like a fawn who hasn't learned the ways of the world yet.

Rome cries out—again with that unfamiliar tinny quality engrained in his outburst.

But Orlando scoops me up in a flash. "No. We're all going to sit down like civilized people. Rome, stand next to the fireplace, like a person. Don't crawl on the floor like an animal. Convince me you are in control of yourself, and you can be near her." Orlando is firm in his ruling as he carries me further into the living room. "You stay there," he instructs me as he lowers my form to sit on the couch. Orlando appears to be the only adult in the room at the moment. He rests his hand on my forehead, looking closely, I'm guessing to search out a lump. "Should I be calling your doctor? Declan was pretty clear that any head injuries are top concern."

I shake my head, wincing at the tension in my cranium. "I really am fine. If I can walk and talk, I don't need to panic." I motion toward the fireplace, where Rome is gripping the edge of the mantle. "Don't worry about me, Orlando. Rome is the one in pain."

Orlando runs his fingers through my hair—a thing I am certain he has never done for any other woman. He saves his tender side for a moment when there are no witnesses, and he knows he can be precious without being seen. "I got blood into him, thanks to you calling when you did. He lost language, Coco. That's dangerous. I'm not sure how much longer he would have lasted like that before attacking. You're very lucky. He's on his way to being himself again. Loads better than he was ten minutes ago, but he's not in control yet. Caution is the name of the game." Orlando rubs the nape of his neck, standing straighter. "I don't understand how this happened."

"I need to go to him," I insist. Though I've only been with Rome for a week now, my heart couldn't care less about things like clinginess or healthy boundaries. My body is screaming to be near him, aching to go to his side to make sure he's alright.

But Orlando turns me on the couch, tucks a throw pillow behind my back and props my feet up, removing my heels. "Not yet."

Orlando rights himself, running a hand over his face as he gears up to deal with Rome.

My boyfriend paces in front of the fireplace with measured steps that I can tell he is struggling to keep in check. His breathing is syncopated, his heartbeat visible in his cheeks. He grips the mantle of the unlit fireplace, his tension illuminated by the light fixture overhead.

Orlando eyes his cousin. "Alright, Rome. You said you would calm down if you could see her. So here she is, plain as day. Now you're going to explain to me whatever it is that did this to you. Start talking, both of you."

I clam up, not wanting to describe a moment that explosive to Orlando, of all people. My private life is private.

Rome watches me with wild side eyes. His hair is standing on end and his clothes are disheveled. He looks like a man undone, which is decidedly better than a man unhinged—as he was however long ago.

My heart breaks for his plight.

Rome breathes heavily through his nose, making a concerted effort to appear normal, though I can tell his body feels like it is coming apart at the seams.

I don't know how I know this, but I can feel his pain. It's not as acutely as he is experiencing it, I'm sure, but to a far lesser degree there is an echo of his agony that rings through my bones. It's akin to intuition.

Just like how I know what Orlando needs when he is having an off day.

My stomach hollows at the thought. I try to push away the notion of me mating with Rome mere months after mating with Orlando. It's not possible. I know it's not.

Then again, it wasn't possible for me, a human, to mate

with Orlando, a vampire. Rome started the mating ritual without meaning to, back when there were still leaves on the trees and hope in my heart.

No, no. I can't mate with Rome. I'm already mated.

But from what I know of vampiric mating (which admittedly isn't much) the hallmarks are there.

I do my best to push away that line of reasoning. "His hand is bleeding, Orlando."

When I point to Rome's left hand, Orlando's mouth tightens. "I'll bandage it up once he's under control." Then he jabs his finger in Rome's direction. "Start talking."

Rome wraps his arms around his middle, physically holding himself together because I am too far away to do it for him. "You know I brought her here because she had a fight with her family. I took her to the guest bedroom to get settled in, and we started making out."

I blanch. Calling what we did simply "making out" cheapens the whole thing. We orchestrated planets. We influenced nature.

Making out is what teenagers do.

"Things started heating up."

I bite down on my lower lip. "When we were together, I started to see... and I felt... and I think Rome..." I clear my throat, my cheeks flushed that this is how this night is playing out.

I want Orlando privy to the details of my bedroom antics about as much as I want a hole in the head.

"I felt it, too," Rome assures me, meeting my gaze with a yearning I cannot ignore a second longer.

Orlando scrunches his eyes shut. "Thanks for the details I don't need in my brain. Get to the part where all the blood drained from you and she started being able to see through walls."

Rome gapes at me. "You did what?"

I shake my head, wishing none of this was happening. I could be curled up in bed with Rome right now if things hadn't gone so awry. "I can't see through walls. When Rome was distressed, I could see him. Like, in my mind's eye. I wanted to be with him, so somehow, I found a way."

Rome stares at me in wonder, his palm flattening over his heart. "Coletta," he coos. It's the most controlled sound he's made thus far. "I'm alright now," he promises, though the hand at his side vibrates with a tremor that doesn't escape my notice. He clenches his fist and then shakes it out. "I'll be fine. Orlando brought me blood. It's just taking its sweet time kicking in."

"Things were getting more intense," I tell Orlando, my voice hoarse with emotion. I would rather bury this conversation forever, but I don't want Rome telling Orlando too many details. "I saw shapes. Blue and silver swirls. Like I was having a hallucination."

"I saw the same thing," Rome confirms, nodding emphatically. "I'm so glad you saw it, too. I didn't think I would be, but I am. This is right. This is what should happen. It's complete. We did it."

Orlando looks positively distressed. "You're happy about this? Well, I'm not! You get what this means, right?"

Rome locks eyes with me, staring in wonder as if we are completely new to each other now. "Once I feed her my blood, we will be mated."

5

MATED

Orlando paces the living room, fretting about something that I have yet to wrap my mind around. My denial runs deep and couples easily with the logic that dismisses this entire thing as a non-possibility.

"Mated," Orlando says again. "This is what you want? This is what you hoped would happen?" He shakes his head. "But Coco and I are mated. I don't understand. I still feel our bond, so that's not gone. She's mated to you, too? What made it possible?"

Rome glues his back to the far wall. He keeps me in his eyeline but makes sure he doesn't come close in case his hands don't remember how to be careful. "I didn't hold back this time," he states simply. "I was afraid to mate with anyone before, but when we were together upstairs, I realized how stupid that was. There's nothing I want more than to be with her—to be good for her. I can't know her completely without the mating ritual giving me the cheat sheet."

Orlando throws his head back. "The loss of blood so suddenly makes sense now. That's part of the ritual."

I frown at him. "No, it's not. You didn't go through that when you gave me your blood that first time."

Orlando keeps his chin from me. "I chugged all the blood I had on hand before I gave you a few drops of my blood to seal the ritual. I don't know a ton about mating, but that's one of the drawbacks. That first time is rough. I was prepared." He pinches the bridge of his nose. "Plus, I didn't start the mating ritual; Rome did. So I was only doing half of it all. I wasn't nearly as depleted. Once Rome gives you his blood to seal you two together, you won't have to see him in your mind's eye. You'll be able to intuit what he needs without having the mental image to guide the way."

I settle into the scratchy throw pillow, my legs still stretched out across the couch. "This barely makes sense." But Rome's confession rings through my bones still. I need to confirm his intentions before another second passes. "You wanted this? You thought this through and made the choice to mate with me?"

Rome's chin moves up and down once, his eyes still wide. "I didn't know it would work, but yes. It's you, Coletta. Only you. Always you. But you have to complete it still. We're nearly sealed."

Insecurity flashes in my eyes. I wish we were alone to discuss this, but I guess we have no secrets from Orlando now. "You aren't going to run?"

Rome melts, though his forearms still have tremors he cannot suppress. "I've never taken a woman to this cabin, tré-sur. Never. I am not the type to invest in a relationship. You know that. But whenever you need something, it's all I can do not to shake the world off its axis to get it for you. This will only help me love you better. I need that." Sincerity radiates off him. "The only thing you have to do is drink my blood. Then we belong to each other forever."

Forever is a grand concept I rarely consider, since my forever is destined to be far shorter than his.

But that doesn't stop me from wanting every bit of him I can get. I melt for this man. I have no other choice. Even though the notion of drinking yet more blood is strange, no part of him could ever be a monster to me. I want no distance between his heart and mine.

"But I'm linked to Orlando," I argue, confused at the liberties nature has taken with things that were supposed to be rules. Somehow those hard and fast lines faded into myth over the decades.

Rome holds my gaze with an intensity I cannot measure. "I don't think that will change. Please, Coletta." He raps his fist against his ribs over his heart. "The mating ritual wants to complete itself. Can't you feel it?"

Of course I feel the ocean of distance between us that yearns to erase itself.

My chin turns to Orlando, who raises his hands in surrender. "Hey, I'm just the guy who delivers the blood. I've got no skin in this game."

That's all the green light I need.

Though I am still unsteady, I ignore the tilting of the room. I stand and stumble toward Rome like a zombie searching for the only pulse left in the world.

It's strange to me how wrong everyone is, assuming Rome doesn't have a heart. They call him cold and cruel, but that's not the man who holds me tenderly and calls me to read me poetry at night.

"Careful," Orlando warns us both. "Easy, Rome. She's breakable, and the blood hasn't been in your system long enough for you to see straight."

To his credit, Rome holds himself back, lifting his tremulous arms to me but waiting for me to come to him. He lowers himself to sit on his butt beside the fireplace. His fingers stretch toward me, practically vibrating with need.

The world feels all wrong when I am on one side of the room, and he is on the other. Obviously, we belong together. Half his angst is because we are so far apart.

When my fingers touch on his, my whole body shudders. My mouth pops open when a blue spark sizzles out from the spot where we are connected. A silver swirl dances five inches out from us, drawing my eyes as wonder consumes me.

"Did you see that? What was that?" I ask Rome.

Maybe I'm asking Orlando.

Perhaps I am asking the universe what it has in store for us before I take this giant step into the unknown.

But sometimes I've learned that you have to leap without all the answers lain out before you. Sometimes that is the only way to know you are truly alive.

Rome pulls me down to sit on his lap. The moment my forehead rests against his cheek, my chin on his shoulder, we exhale in unison.

"That was us, tré-sur. Just us."

Rome's lips touch on mine, and the world finally rights itself.

His arms only settle when they are holding me. After hours of turbulence, ours hearts begin a steady rhythm of comforting each other.

I could get used to this.

Orlando shuffles to Rome's side, catching my eye with a glint of silver from his dagger. My inhale is sharp until I realize Orlando's intent.

The knife nicks the heel of Rome's hand, and suddenly the rest of the world disappears into the periphery. No smell, sight or sound holds my attention like that small prick of blood. It pools on Rome's skin in fat droplets meant only for me.

Intuition tells me this blood is mine while my mouth fills with saliva.

Orlando's blood in my tea made food taste right again. It was the best part of my day because it was made for me, filling in the gaps where my own body's chemistry fell short.

This drop of blood calls to me in the same way, except for the lust that falls over me like a veil. It shrouds me from logical thought that would argue how unsafe, unsanitary and unreasonable it is to drink blood from another person.

Rome lets me volley with the choice, but I hardly have one to make. Longing is a tame descriptor for the thirst that sends a flame of agony up my throat.

My lips mold around the heel of Rome's hand. My tongue laves over the blood, welcoming it into my body— for better or worse.

6

CONNECTIONS

The wintry cold cocoons us in the cabin, sealing the world outside and all its problems far away from our happy haven.

"What would you say if I told you I am never leaving this bed?" I ask lazily. I fully intend to remain sprawled across the sheets of the guest bedroom for as long as humanly possible. I keep thinking I will get tired of having no schedule and basically being horizontal with Rome throughout most of my waking moments, but after a week of giving in to every imaginable desire, I see no end in sight.

Rome lifts my foot and kisses my toes, knowing exactly what that does to a woman. "Good. Then I've got you right where I want you." He kisses my ankle, giving me a devilish look when his mouth suctions around the spot behind my ankle, which he knows will start my engine all over again.

I grip the pillow, my back arching as my eyes roll with delight. "Is this how good you normally are in bed, or is it the bond that tells you exactly what I need?"

"I like to think it's a little of both. My ego needs to believe that, at least." Rome's lips trail slowly upward as he hooks my ankle over his shoulder, kissing his way up the length of my leg. "This is my favorite weather," he comments, rubbing the muscle of my thigh while he nips at the inside of my knee.

"What is? The tropics of this sweaty bedroom or the snow outside?"

"The snow. There are fewer people outside causing trouble. The world is quieter."

I chew on my lower lip while he works his magic on my leg. "I like that."

We have the shades open because there is no one around for miles. We can be naked in full view of the second-story window without shame or fear of being found out. We can be together in the daylight, warm while watching the snow fall outside.

I am firm in my conviction that I never want to leave this bed.

An unfamiliar sound interrupts his hand crawling further up the inside of my thigh. My brows furrow. "Your phone is on? That's new."

Rome pinches the swell of my hip before he puts my leg down on the sheet. "I turned it on while you were in the shower this morning. It's been a week that we've been gone, little cannoli. As much as I want to pretend I can leave things without supervision, that's not always possible." He answers his phone, sitting naked on the side of the bed. "Yeah?"

I watch the ropes of tension cording his back as the conversation progresses. Though I don't know what Orlando is saying, I have little faith that it's all been sunshine and roses while we've been away. Last night, I had a phantom ache in my arm, but there was no cause for it. My intuition kicked in, letting me know that Orlando's arm was hurting him.

After a few back and forths, Rome ends the call, pushing out the concern creasing his brow with a forced smile in my direction. "Where were we?" He makes to reach for my leg, but I sit up, drawing my knees to the side.

"Is Orlando's arm okay?"

Rome sucks his lower lip into his mouth. "You're still connected to him, huh. He's alright."

"You don't know that," I argue. "You didn't even ask him."

"Orlando would have told me if he was injured."

I shoot him a look of disbelief. "I hope you heard what a lie that was." I hold out my hand, not satisfied until his phone is in my hand. "Orlando?" I say when the call connects. "Is your arm okay?"

The pause is not reassuring. "It's alright. You felt that, did you?"

"I didn't mean to. What happened?"

Orlando's voice is warm, settling into a rich baritone he uses to reassure me when life turns things on its head. "We broke up a halluci-den and I took a baseball bat to the arm. It's not broken. Everything is fine. The bruising will be gone in a day, if that."

"Okay." Though as I say this, I feel anything but okay when I know my big sweetie pie is injured. But this is his life, so I know I need to develop a thicker skin about the whole thing.

"My blood still doing what it needs to for you?"

I nod. "Yeah."

"I figured we were still mated. You have enough of my blood left to last you the week?"

"I do."

"Good. I gotta go, Colette my dove."

My cheeks pink. I've never delivered our tease of a greeting with no clothes on. Even though he can't see me, I am aware of the scandal. "Stay safe, Orlando my love."

He snickers and then ends the call.

I hand the phone back to Rome with guilt darkening my features.

"It's okay that you're still mated to Orlando," Rome

supplies, sizing up my insecurity with a firmness all his own. He is determined that everything will be okay, and we will not devolve into a fight about this thing we cannot control. "It's good, actually. You're healthier than ever. Makes the acrobatics we got into last night possible." His eyebrows bounce a few times, trying to inject a touch of levity into the mix.

I would have thought completing the mating ritual with Rome would push out the connection I have to Orlando, but that hasn't been the case. We're still in a trial-and-error phase, but so far it seems I need Orlando's blood to keep my body fully functional.

Rome's blood has had an unintended effect I haven't quite found the language to talk about. It's always me who doesn't have the guts to verbalize the unknown.

I am healing faster than I normally would, but I haven't told either of them that. It shouldn't be a secret, but the newness of it all makes me want to hold it tight to the vest. I don't know what it means that since I started drinking Rome's blood once a day, as well as Orlando's, that the scrape I got on my knee two nights ago is completely gone.

Like it never happened.

No, I don't want to tell Rome about that until I know what it means.

I guess I haven't changed completely. I am still guarded, constantly aware that one oddity too many could push away the person I love for good.

Rome presses his lips together, feathering his fingers through mine. "True confessions?"

"Well, they're the best kind."

"I'm a little bummed that it's not my blood that makes you stronger." When I open my mouth to reassure him that it's our love that makes me strong, too, Rome holds up his hand to stop my heart from bleeding out on the bed between us. "It's fine. Just a little hit to my pride. Probably a good thing. Might be dysfunctional my way."

I motion around the cabin we haven't left for a week. "I think we passed functional a long time ago, pal."

Rome snorts at my accurate assessment. "Fair enough."

When my phone rings, I almost don't recognize my own ringtone. It's been so long since I touched the thing.

My brows furrow. "I turned my phone off a week ago. That's weird."

Rome raises his hand. "I turned it on while you were in the shower. I thought you might want to call your brother. Plus, we agreed to check in with the real world once a week."

I frown at the time lapse while I grab up my phone. I swear as I check the caller ID. "It's my father. I don't want to hear from him."

Rome kisses my forehead. "If you don't talk to him, I will."

I groan, knowing that would go over horribly. "Fine. I'll talk to him, but I'm not going to like it."

7

OVERDUE PHONE CALL

"Yeah?" I say to my father when the call connects.

The sheriff exhales. "Your mailbox is full."

"That's the thing about not wanting to hear from anyone. Well, it's your grand moment. Here I am. You caught me before I turn off my phone again."

"Colette, don't be like this. Or if you're going to be like this, don't disappear on us. You've been gone for a week. Let's talk about it."

I manage a dry laugh that sounds more bitter than joyful as I tug a sheet over my chest to cover myself. "Can't blame me for turning out exactly like you. We don't talk about things. We get far away from each other when there's a family emergency."

The sheriff sighs but doesn't protest my attitude. "I'd rather you tell me how I failed than stay silent. Let it out."

"Let what out?" I rage as I cast around for clothing. I don't want to be naked while I am talking to my father. "The fact that for two years, the three of you had a secret from me? The fact that you have cancer? The fact that you've got a few weeks left, and I'm only just hearing about it all now?" I shake my head. "I'm telling you, the best thing I can do for our relationship is let you go without me around. That's how you wanted it. That's how you orchestrated it. If you don't want me around for your life, then you don't get me around for your death."

"That's fair," the sheriff replies when I go silent. "I'm not asking you to hold my hand on my deathbed or anything. I know I messed up."

The mental image of my father in a hospital, holding my hand while he breathes his last rattles my insides with horror.

"You did this," I seethe. "Declan is all I have in our family, and you made him keep a secret from me. Our friendship is precious to me. He is the only one of you three who actually loves me, and you broke it. Why? Would it have been so horrible to treat me like I'm part of the family? Do you hate me that much?"

The sheriff's voice is quiet. "I don't hate you, Coco. I love you."

More bitter laughter spills from me with no end in sight. Rome tugs on his underwear and backs away, leaving me to a conversation neither of us wants him to witness. I don't want to be the angry person in his mind, but this isn't a conversation I can endure with a smile on my face.

My father's insistence sounds sincere. "I know that sounds fake, but it's not. Would you believe that parenting is hard?"

"No, I wouldn't. I wasn't around you for years, which made your job a piece of cake, because you bowed out of it altogether." I shrug into Rome's white dress shirt because I think we discarded my clothes in the living room last. "What is it about me that makes you like this? You talk to Fintan. You're nice to Declan. Why do you hate me?"

"I don't hate you, Coco. I hate me."

My mouth slams shut because I don't understand.

My father takes my pause as an invitation to come clean. "I hate myself because no matter how hard I try, I can't save you. Another note, Coco. Fintan found another note taped to your salon's door this week. No matter how many patrol cars I send to Midtown, I can't stop the revolution from coming after you. I couldn't stop them from targeting your mother. She had a hard life because of them. Now they want your blood, and I can't figure out who is behind it all. I can't put a stop to this. I failed your mother, and now I've failed you." He lets loose a grunt of frustration. "And now that I am dying, the only thing that haunts me about my own death is that I won't be around to stop them anymore."

I want to break things. I don't have words or coherent thoughts. I want to take a baseball bat and shatter anything that dares stand unbroken.

I am broken, and part of me might remain that way for as long as I live.

I don't need to empathize with the sheriff. He made a series of wrong decisions. But when I open my mouth, I realize I am my brother's sister, because Declan's wisdom sneaks out of me when I should shout at my father to go away and save his sadness for someone who cares. "You are not responsible for stopping a revolution. And you didn't fail Mom. Her genetics failed her."

The sheriff's voice catches. "Maybe so, but there's not a day that goes by that I don't wonder if I could have done better. If I could have cracked down harder. If I should have taken her away from Mayfield so she didn't have to be so close to the chaos. I didn't do it right with her, so I tried a different way with you, which made it all worse." His cadence sounds like he is tired. "You had a good life in Lonmure, once you got on your feet. Both branches of your salon over there are thriving. Telling you about my condition would have been selfish because I know what you would have done."

I grip my phone. "I would have flown to Mayfield and made you go to a doctor with some sort of miracle cure! I would have stayed on top of your appointments and treatments. I would have had a say in how this played out. If you had let me in, maybe you wouldn't be on death's door right now!"

Of all things, the sheriff chuckles. "You don't think I know that? I didn't tell you because you deserve a good life. After how hard you worked to build your business, I know you would have given it all up and flown home to be with me. That wouldn't be right, so I made that decision for you. Once again, maybe it was the wrong call, but I stand by it. I got to watch my girl thrive. I have a whole collection of articles about your salon on my computer."

I snort. "I wasn't aware you knew how to turn on your computer."

The sheriff chuckles. "Ha, ha. Declan set up one of those fancy alerts that tells my phone whenever there's an article written about you on the internet. Every day I missed my little girl, I knew you were out there, killing it in the world because I wasn't selfish with you. I didn't weigh you down with my problems because you'd been through enough of your own. Wrong call or not—I stand by it. I'll go to my grave regretting a lot of things, but not once will I go back on that one. Staying away so you could have a good life is the one solid thing I did for you. So don't ask me to apologize for keeping you in the dark for two years; I would only be lying if I did."

My mouth falls open as several splutters and half-sentences come out.

He didn't tell me because he wanted me to have a good life?

I mean, sure, if he had told me two years ago, the Kennedy Salon wouldn't have been successful. I was still doing most of the work myself back then, trying to get the business off the ground.

My mouth pulls to the side. "You sent me away when I was fifteen. You got your cancer diagnosis eight years after you sent me away."

The sheriff grumbles incoherently before he chooses his words. "Well, that part, I'll apologize for. Those first eight years are my fault. The last two, well, those are fate's fault."

My reply comes out in a rasp. "I would have come home for you. If only you wanted me there, I would have left my business and stayed by your side."

The sheriff's voice warms. "I know you would have. You're a good daughter, even if I was a crap father. You can be mad all you want, and I'm sorry things went sound the way they did. I wasn't expecting to be given such a grim prognosis. Makes a man think on how he could have lived his life better. Regrets are a heavy thing to carry around."

I want to ask him what he regrets, but part of me knows it's not my place to ask, nor will it fix anything between us.

The sheriff clears his throat. "Declan chewed me out nice and good last night. He's furious with me for breaking what you two have. Said he called you about a million times, but you won't answer."

"I turned my phone off. What you're going through is a family matter, and you made it clear by not telling me about your cancer that I am not part of your family. Noble reasons or not, you cut me out." I sit on the edge of the bed. "And Declan can bite me."

"I've asked for precious little from you because I know I've got no right. But if you have any duty or love or sympathy for me at all, you will call Declan and make up. Let me rest in peace with the knowledge that I didn't ruin the one good thing in your life."

I run my tongue over my top row of teeth. "That's a low blow, Sheriff, tugging on my heartstrings like you've got a right."

He chortles at my upset. "And I want the address of the place you're staying. I won't give it to anyone, and I won't come there. But if things go south before you get back, the boys are going to need to get ahold of you for arrangements and whatnot."

My stomach churns. "I don't want to talk about your funeral arrangements. I haven't even processed what a colossal ass you are. Don't talk about caskets or burials or any of it. You didn't want me in your life; I'll stay away from your death."

The sheriff pauses. "Fine. But I still want your address. Never mind. I got it."

"Huh?"

"You don't think I'm tracing this call? I may not know how to use my computer at home all that well, but I know my way around precinct tech. There. Written on the notepad on the fridge for the boys to find when they need it. Like I said, I'm not coming to see you."

I shake my head slowly as I try to understand how we got to this point in our lives. "You have never made a lick of sense to me. You know that, right?"

The sheriff snorts. "I could say the same of you. But one thing I'm going to say is that I'm damn proud of you, little girl. We don't do the whole mushy thing, but I don't care. I'm proud of you for fighting. For holding your head up. For believing Mayfield could be better, even though there's no evidence to support that."

I swallow hard, unsure what to do with a direct compliment from the man who always overlooks me. "Uh, okay."

"Are you alright where you are? That looks like the middle of the woods, from what I can tell on my phone."

I roll my eyes at him. "I'm fine. I don't mind being alone."

I don't care if this is confessions time with the sheriff; I am not telling him about Rome. That would be the heart attack I can see coming from miles away.

"You're like me, I hate to say." He pauses, his voice softening. "Don't be like me."

All volume deserts me, so I swallow any reply I might be able to conjure and close my eyes. "Goodbye, Sheriff."

8

FAIRFAX, FRANK AND FATHERHOOD

Rome's forte in the kitchen is handmade gnocchi with a red sauce. He whistles while he makes it. I love watching him in the kitchen, especially clad only in his designer boxer briefs that cling to his perfect backside. What a beautiful sight he is.

His phone calls are taking most of the evening because he is actually making them. I am being a giant chicken, so I've only called the salons to make sure all is well with them.

Rome talks on the phone while he stirs the sauce in the pan. "That makes sense. Any idea if this Fairfax fellow is the one who's making the halluci-blend, or if he's another in the chain of people who work for the root of the problem?"

I don't know the answer Rome gets, but it doesn't seem

to please him, so I keep quiet and gather information from my spot on the stool at the kitchen counter.

I know that name. Fairfax. I don't remember where I heard it. Probably a client at the salon. I see a lot of names on the appointment book. Maybe that's it.

"I guess we'll figure out who's at the root of the problem when we deal with Fairfax. Then either the drugs will disappear, or they'll keep leaking into the West End. Take Nico and his crew with you when you go to rescue Frank's kid. Nico will do just about anything to rescue a hurt kid. You'll want someone unhinged with you when you go in. Nico's your man." Rome pauses for a beat. "I'll tell her."

I love how controlled he is, even while on vacation and dealing with a kidnapping.

He told me about the owner of Frank's Grill having his son abducted, so Frank would be forced to push halluci-blend onto the populace. Makes me sick to my stomach, knowing there is a child out there in need of a rescue.

Rome will handle it. He always does.

When Rome ends the call, he sets his phone down on the counter, going back to the sauce as if nothing pulled him out of our blissful haze.

Man, he's good.

"You're staring," Rome comments, his back to me.

"Can you blame me?"

He angles his chin over his shoulder to smirk at me. "There you go, inflating my ego. Careful. It's dangerously large to begin with."

My brows dance mischievously. "You're telling me." I munch on a carrot stick while I try not to think about the phone call with my father, or the child still in need of rescue.

"Orlando says to tell you everything is fine at your house. He'll be up to give you more blood tomorrow afternoon, if all goes well for him tonight."

"Okay." I pick up another carrot stick. "That name you said on the phone. Fairfax. I've heard it before."

"Oh, yeah?"

"Not sure where. Maybe they came into the salon for a haircut. But I've seen or heard the name somewhere." I swallow hard, not wanting to get into work talk with him, but also wanting to be apprised of the big happenings in the West End. "You think Fairfax is the person who abducted Frank's son?"

"One and the same. We've been working on Frank for a while, trying to get him to give up the name." He lowers his voice. "Fairfax sent Frank a box with the boy's little finger in it, so he finally talked. Told Orlando where their drop-offs usually are."

My stomach sours as I close my eyes against the horror. "Oh my gosh."

"That was a few days ago. Orlando got the plates of the guy who delivered the halluci-blend to Frank. He followed him around until he caught the bastard loading halluci-blend into his trunk last night. The address is registered to someone with the last name of Fairfax. Orlando is doing more digging today. They're going to strike tomorrow night, if they are sure that's where the trail ends. They're trying to figure that out now and get a team together. We need to get that kid out, so we have to be sure we're busting into the right place. Otherwise, they might get spooked and do away with the kid altogether."

I lower my head. "Poor Frank. Poor little boy. I can't imagine."

Rome keeps his back to me. "Yes, you can. That's why I didn't want to talk to you about it. But I also don't want to keep secrets from you. I don't know if it was the right thing to do, letting you listen in on that conversation, telling you the details today, but it's what's going on."

I swallow hard. "Thanks for telling me. You're right; I want to know what's going on." I press my lips together, mulling over the name Fairfax a few times, in case the repetition jogs my memory. "Do you think the members of the revolution are the same as the people behind the halluci-blend? I mean, they have the same goal: to destroy vampires."

Rome nods. "I've thought that for a while. But I don't know for sure. The thing about the revolution is that if you cut the head off the monster—kill the person in charge—it won't stop anything. The monster will only grow another head. There's no shortage of people in the world who want to see vampires become a thing of the past. But if this Fairfax person is also a revolutionary, I wouldn't be surprised. It would be a big deal if we took him out. Cleaning up the West End can't truly happen if halluci-blend keeps destroying my people."

"Agreed." I tilt my head to the side while I watch him cook. "Did I ever tell you that I think you're heroic?"

Rome snorts. "You called me a lot of things last night, but I don't recall 'hero' being one of them."

"Well, you are."

Rome shakes his head. "I don't know what sort of agony it is to be a father, since I'll never be one myself, but I can imagine Frank has been through enough torment for one lifetime. If Orlando can find Frank's son and take down Fairfax, that will be a big win, at least for Frank. At this point, I'm not sure which I care about more—ending the stream of halluci-blend coming into the West End that's destroying my people, or saving one small boy from his kidnapper."

I climb off my stool at the counter and cross the kitchen, winding my arms around my boyfriend so I can hold him from behind. "You are a good man, Rome Valentino."

Rome's arm rests atop mine. "No. I'm a man who hasn't

been able to rescue this kid for months, and it's killing me."

I don't know how to quell his angst, so I don't try. I simply hold him tight, assuring Rome with my embrace that I will stay with him, even when he doesn't have the answers.

9

ROME'S BLOOD

Rome cooks in silence after I resume my spot on the stool at the kitchen counter. The grim mood has broken a little while we do our best not to let the messy parts of the world we cannot control ruin our wintry haven. He stirs the sauce while I make notes on the things I need to take care of when I start making my phone calls.

Which I am not up for yet.

The world will always be there, needing me for something. But I don't want to go back to it right now. I'm on what feels like a honeymoon with Rome. A whole week of nothing but bubble baths and feeding each other in between bouts of time together between the sheets.

I hate that my father kept this big a secret. No matter how I try to distract myself, my mind keeps bouncing back to that frustration.

His words echo in my mind, haunting me because I

don't know how to apply them. I can still hear his gruff cadence saying, "Don't be like me."

I set my pen down beside the notebook Rome gave me to scribble in, making an executive decision not to let history repeat itself.

I don't have to be like my father.

I don't have to keep Rome out of the scarier parts of my life.

I clear my throat, summoning courage as best I can. "I have a secret," I announce.

Rome's spine stiffens, but to his credit, his voice stays light. "Is that so? Do you want to tell me what it is?"

"No. But I don't want to end up like my father even more than I don't want to tell you stuff that worries me, so here we go." I suck in a long breath before I begin. "Your blood isn't making me healthier. Orlando's takes care of that. But your blood isn't exactly doing nothing."

I have Rome's full attention now. He sets down the wooden spoon and turns to face me, crossing his arms over his chest while he leans his butt against the counter. "Go on."

I pick the pen back up just so I have something with which I can fiddle. "Two nights ago, I got up in the night to go to the bathroom. I didn't want to turn the lamp on because you were sleeping so soundly." I chew on my lower lip, trying to find the right words. "I tripped over my stiletto that I left in the middle of the floor and fell. I got a scratch on my knee that was bleeding a little bit."

Rome launches himself away from the counter and races to my side. He's so cute—his brows furrowed and his fingers tracing over my knees while he examines me for a fatal injury. "Are you okay? Why would you keep that from me? How did I not notice? I didn't even hear you fall."

"You aren't exactly coherent after sex," I remind him.

How I love this man. I lean forward and kiss his forehead, cupping his cheeks because I can't not. He's too cute to resist.

"I'm fine. It was a scrape. By morning it should have been a bruise. I went to the bathroom and staunched the blood. No big deal. I was going to grab a band-aid in the morning. But when the sun rose, there wasn't a bruise, and the scrape was a tiny line, like it had been healing for days. But it had only been a handful of hours."

"That's why you wore pants two days ago. I thought you were chilly, so I turned up the heat."

"No, I didn't want my blood around you."

"Makes sense." Rome's lips purse as he tries to puzzle through what I am saying to him. "I don't understand. You're okay, right? Why didn't you tell me you hurt yourself?"

"I was going to tell you when you woke up, but by morning, there was no need. The injury was practically gone."

His head bobs. "Okay. That's good, then, right?"

I love the feeling of his fingers on my knee. "Sure, it's good, but it's also not possible. I shouldn't be healed that quick. It was a pretty rough scrape."

He tilts his head to the side, trying to make sense of my words.

I lower my voice, as if I am afraid someone might overhear the scandal of something good happening for me. "Rome, it's your blood. That's the only way I can explain it. Orlando's blood changed me. It made me healthy, but I didn't have vampire healing." I study Rome's fingers on my knee. "But now that I'm drinking your blood too, I heal like a vampire."

Rome's nose crinkles, but then his eyes widen as my words bring about the intended revelation, finally putting us on the same page. "Are you serious? My blood is turning you into a vampire?"

My nose scrunches at the left turn. "What?"

Rome grabs my hand and drags me toward the door. "Let's get back to the city. Declan can fly with you to Lonmure. Your doctor needs to look at you." Fear rounds his eyes. "Not your doctor. We can't have anyone finding out about this. If you morph into a vampire, they'll turn on you. You'll lose everything. We'll talk to Declan. He can figure this out. He can undo it."

My bare feet slow. I'm still only wearing his dress shirt and am hardly ready to leave the cabin. "Rome, that's not what's happening. I'm not turning into a vampire. Your blood is enhancing me. It's giving me something useful, but I'm still me."

"How can you tell?"

I scratch my elbow. "Well, I don't crave random blood, only yours and Orlando's. I think that would be the dead giveaway."

Rome pauses, his shoulders lowering. "I guess that's true." He squeezes my hand. "I still want Declan to give you a look. This is uncharted territory, Coletta. We're not skipping anything important."

I nod. "When Declan and I are talking again, I'll ask him what he thinks."

Rome's lips press together in a firm line. "Don't think I didn't hear you skirt around what I'm asking you to do. Talking with Declan eventually isn't the same as having a medical exam."

I cross my arms over my chest. "Look, I'm fine. I feel great. Better than I've ever been. This is good news, not a reason to panic."

Rome softens, palming my cheek. "Oh, tré-sur. Loving you means every tiny scratch is a reason to panic."

I step into his body's space and run my hands up his bare chest. "Did you turn the stove off?"

He kisses my lips just once. "Yes. Why?"

"Good." I lean up on my toes and kiss the firmness

away from his lips, replacing it with malleable sweetness he does not possess unless I give it to him.

Rome's arms curve around me, holding me to him so he can peruse my body as thoroughly as he pleases.

Oh, how he pleases me. I love this sweet escape, where time means little, and problems are even less important. I never want to leave this cabin.

I tuck my thumbs into the band of Rome's underwear, tracing the dip of his hips just because I can.

His tongue finds mine, letting me know that we haven't made love on the floor of the foyer in a while. His kiss deepens, giving my body something to rally around. His hands slide up my naked legs, tracing my hips underneath the white shirt of his that I love wearing like a dress.

"Do you like when I cook for you?" he asks in a husky whisper.

"Yes." I love the way my body feels against his.

"Do you like the way I make love to you?"

"I can't remember. You'll have to show me again. Then I can tell you if I like it."

Rome chuckles darkly into our kiss. "I'm going to make you pay for that little remark."

"Mm. I look forward to it."

I have him right where my thriving libido wants him.

When the lights go out around us, for a second, I assume Rome has found the switch and turned it off to enhance the mood. But when Rome stiffens, he ends the kiss and holds me tight to his front. "Stinking cabin. I'll go check the fuse box."

I kiss him below his jawline behind his ear, letting him know that I don't need electricity at this exact moment. "We don't need lights for what I had in mind for you."

Rome chortles quietly, his thumb sweeping over me in ways that make me shudder. "You might be singing a different tune when we freeze over. It's winter outside, little cannoli. I'll be right back. Hold that thought."

But he doesn't get more than a few feet away before the doorknob jiggles.

10

INTRUDERS

The intrusive sound of the doorknob rattling lights a fire up my spine, sending me scampering away from the entrance toward the place where Rome stands, his fists clenched.

"Go hide upstairs in the bedroom," he warns me in the darkness. "Where did I put my pants? Where's my gun?"

I can't remember the last time he used either of those items. "No idea. I'll call the sheriff," I tell him, running as soundlessly as I can toward the stairs. While normally I would be readying to defend my territory against an intruder, I am unarmed and not properly clothed, so I get away from the entrance as fast as I can. I try to remember the floorplan of the cabin, so I don't trip and fall along the way.

I snatch up my phone from the kitchen and the run to the stairs. My fingers skip over the banister while I race up the steps. I hate that I can't see anything. It's nighttime, and there's no electricity. I hope my phone has a charge.

I locate the bedroom and do my best to let the moonlight lead the way. The shade is still open, letting a faint illumination inside. Though I can't see much, I make out the outline of Rome's pants. My phone finds my hand while I wonder where on earth Rome might have stashed his gun.

When the call connects, I cringe at the hope in my father's voice. "Coco! I can't believe you called. I'm so glad."

I don't have time for pleasantries. While it doesn't sound like the intruder made their way into the house just yet, I know my time is limited. "Who did you tell where we were staying? Who did you give the address to?"

"What? No one. Who's 'we'? I thought you were there alone."

I grimace at the slip, but breeze past in hopes he doesn't latch onto it. "You got my location this morning and now someone cut the power to the cabin. They're trying to get in the front door. Who did you tell?"

"No one! Coco, I swear. I didn't tell anyone. I went to the grocery store after I talked to you today. I've been home ever since."

I touch my forehead. "I'm so mad, I can't think straight. Call local law enforcement and send over a detail. I can't find a gun, and someone is trying to get inside!"

The sheriff's calm is disheveled, but he slips into work

mode easily enough. "Okay. I'm calling it in right now. Look around you. Anything can be used as a weapon."

I end the call, chewing on my lower lip because he is right. I need to find a way to arm myself. To arm Rome.

Where would Rome hide his gun?

He doesn't like being vulnerable, and I am standing in the room where he has been most exposed.

It's got to be in here.

If I had doubts that Rome and I are the same wild animal, they are put to rest when it takes me all of ten seconds to find his gun, which he stashed in the drawer of the nightstand on his side of the bed.

I haven't heard the crash of a breech yet, so I race through the hall and flit down the stairs in the dark. I bang my hip on the table and nearly hurtle over the couch to get to Rome, but I manage to make it to the living room just in time.

The door flings open, revealing a man holding a gun, with an accomplice behind him. My heart stutters in my chest, but I manage to keep my wits about me. Thanks to Orlando's blood and Rome's, my hands are steady, even if I feel like I am about to fall apart on the inside.

Both intruders have black ski masks pulled over their visage, obscuring their identities. The first one in has a gun, which is aimed directly at the unarmed Rome.

A bleat of terror is all I permit myself before the good old family instinct takes over.

This is why the sheriff took me shooting when I was young.

This is why I don't have any qualms about defending my territory. I know that if I don't, the revolutionaries will take me yet again.

I will not be the helpless waif in somebody's basement.

I don't hesitate, but pull the gun up and fire. I would be frustrated if someone else took a shot with my gun, but I don't have the time for proper firearm protocol. A weapon is aimed at the man I love.

Nothing else exists, except for my need to take this criminal out.

My ears are ringing, but I don't flinch. The first body drops, but the second is retreating. Even though he is armed, apparently the sight of Rome in his underwear and me wearing only Rome's shirt is too damning a scene for him to take with a clear head.

Though I am barefoot and clad in only Rome's shirt, I dart after the second intruder, stepping on the writhing body of my victim while Rome arrests the fallen man's weapon.

"Colette, stay here!" Rome orders, but I am not interested in letting the second intruder get away.

Though it is snowing outside and I am barefoot, that matters little to my hyper-focused mind. All I want is to take down the person who interrupted our perfect haven and brought the drama of Mayfield to our doorstep.

I am not going to live like this—constantly on edge and never allowed to take an actual break from all that the world demands of me.

I stop running so I can steady my aim, pointing my gun at the man fleeing to his car. He parked down the road, giving me a clear enough shot as he runs unobstructed.

Hitting a moving target is not my forte, but when the shot fires, I am grateful to have hit his leg.

Good. Limp around for a while, dummy.

I take another shot because he is still ambling toward his car. My jaw tightens because now he is too far away for a true shot to be aimed effectively. I point Rome's gun at his car instead, shooting out the window. I am trying to pierce the tire, but I only manage to shatter the back side window before he drives off, no doubt leaving a trail of blood and disappointment behind him.

My lips firm with displeasure. I should have taken another shot.

Rome's footsteps are nearly silent in the snow, but his presence is so attuned to mine that I know he is there before I turn around. "Coletta, you're barefoot. Give me the gun, tré-sur. Come here."

It's then that I realize I can't feel my feet.

Rome seems to understand this. He is bare-chested, but at least has pants on now, plus shoes, which is a step up from my lack of attire. He gently takes the gun from my grip, putting on the safety and pocketing the thing. Then he scoops me up in his arms like only the best dashing vampire princes know how to do, and carries me inside.

We aren't safe anymore, but we're together. The only warmth I can feel is that one truth, which promises me there are better days to come.

11

NEW LIVING ARRANGEMENTS

I hate that our beautiful time together is ending like this. But after our hideaway was compromised, there aren't many other options. We either leave now, or we take our chances and wait for more revolutionaries to find us.

Both feel like terrible options.

But I don't mention that while I get dressed in clean clothes after the hot shower Rome insisted I take. Part of his emphatic reasoning was because I just ran outside in the snow after our attacker in nothing but his shirt. Frostbite is a very real concern.

But the real reason I know he wants me to take a shower is so I don't have to hear him extracting information from the man I shot. The water warms and cleanses me, shielding me from any screaming coming from the main floor that might haunt my dreams.

I shot a man. I shot him because he came after my boyfriend.

Self-loathing washes itself down the drain even after I turn off the water and wrap myself in the towel.

The police are on their way here, thanks to the sheriff calling in the breech, so I don't dawdle as I pull on the jeans Orlando packed for me. I tug the cashmere pink sweater over my head and wind my long brown waves into a high bun.

It's quiet downstairs, which I know means that the intruder has died. I can only hope Rome extracted enough information from him before his final breath. We need to know what we are up against.

Rome's footsteps are easy to pick out as he trots up the stairs. I flinch at the blood dripping from his fingers. "Are you alright?" we ask each other in unison, and then exhale a little lightness together.

I hold up my hands. "I'm fine. Hopefully that's the last person I'll ever have to shoot. Though, I said that the last time I fired my weapon." I shrug. "One of these days, it'll be true."

Rome's shoulders lower. "I'm sorry you had to do that. Good for you for finding my gun so quickly. Might have had an entirely different outcome if you hadn't acted as you did." His jaw ticks with tension. "The bullets they had loaded weren't dipped in your blood, so they were coming for you, not for me."

Though I suspected as much, it still smites me across the ribcage, kindling resentment and rage that might never fully go away.

At least it's a pain with which I am well familiar.

Rome grants me a somber bow of his head and tries to slip past me as if he's got something to hide. "I need a few minutes before we talk about our next move."

My nose scrunches. "What's wrong?"

Rome's neck shrinks. "I don't like that my hands are bloody around you." He shakes his head. "I don't like that any of this happened."

To make a point that we are one, I follow him into the bathroom and get out a fresh towel. "I'm not scared of you or of how you handle things. I am the one who fired the first shot, if you recall. All I see when I look at you is the man who protected me." I turn on the tap and squirt soap into his palms.

He keeps his eyes from me while he scrubs himself clean. "I hate that you had to protect me. If he'd gotten in a shot, I could have been injured long enough for them to take you." His head swings in my direction, his chin resting on the crown of my head while he washes his hands. "Thank you."

"Don't think on it another second. It's you and me, Rome. We are well within our rights to defend the house when someone breaks in."

"I'm not sure the police will see it that way."

"Well, you'll have to hide out up here, then. I'll deal with the police. I know that if they find a vampire on the premise, the investigation will be skewed." I hate saying those words, but it doesn't make them any less true. "I'll handle it."

Rome kisses the top of my head. "Thanks. I'll finish washing up, and then I'll pack us up."

My lips press together. "We're going back to Mayfield?"

"I'm not sure we have another choice. We have to strike now."

"What does that mean?" I turn off the water for him once his hands are clean.

Rome's tone turns grave. "The man you shot? That was Steven Fairfax. The man who kidnapped Frank's son is dead now, and I've got the address of his hideout. It's not the house Orlando and Nico hit. He's got the boy stashed at a separate location. No idea if the guy who got away will make it back to Mayfield, but if he does, there goes our window for rescuing the kid."

"Call Orlando!" I tell him as worry rises in my chest. "He can rescue the boy now before the revolutionaries figure out which way is up. We have to act fast!"

Rome kisses my cheek. "I did, little cannoli. He's on his way with Nico and his crew. They're going to get the boy out, but they can't take him to his father until we clear out the place. We need somewhere we can keep the boy and his father until it's safe for them to walk around without a target on their backs. Getting them out is one job. Keeping them safe so they aren't gunned down is another."

I gnaw on my lower lip. "My house," I suggest.

Rome shakes his head. "You know I'm not going to say yes to that. The revolutionaries tracked us here to hunt you down. Your house isn't safe." He takes off his clothes and lets them pool on the tile. "You're not going to like my suggestion."

I try not to let his beautiful body distract me from the conversation. "Let's hear it."

He turns on the shower and steps in, wetting his hair while he draws the curtain shut so I can focus on his words. "I want you to stay with either your father or Declan. Even Fintan would be fine. Just until we get this taken care of. This is it, Coletta. This is the root of the halluci-blend coming into the West End. These are also the people behind the threats on your life. I'm sure more will always pop up, but for now, this is the head of the snake, and I need to cut it off."

I feign a swoon. "You're so poetic when you're gruesome."

He manages a heavy chuckle. "I mean it, Coletta. I want you safe and not in your house. I don't want anyone to be able to find you until we have a better handle on the situation." He pauses before he presses into my emotional wound. "I know that if my father was dying, I would want to spend every second I could with him—whether he deserved my company or not."

I take in his heavy-handed suggestion without brushing it off, as I very much would like to do. "My relationship with the sheriff has been dead for a decade. There's no point in pretending otherwise. If he wanted me around, he would have made that happen any time in the past ten years."

Rome's shower is quick, but despite all we've just experienced, he is remarkably clear-headed. "You mean like him telling you about his situation now? Or how about him trying to institute family dinners? What about him coming into the salon to see you?"

I chew on my lower lip as I pack up our toiletries. "I think it's a waste of everyone's time, but if you really feel this strongly about it, then I guess I can make nice with the sheriff."

Rome turns off the water and comes out of the shower, toweling his body and stealing my focus. "I would like it very much. You need to move in there. Just for a day or two."

"Wait, what? You want me to *stay* at the sheriff's house?"

"It's the safest place. Elias knows how to defend his territory. Plus, no one is stupid enough to try to break into the sheriff's home. If you hide out there for a day or two, we'll have Frank's son out and can get him somewhere safe. Then my weak points will be secured, so I can go after everyone involved in Fairfax's operation." He tugs on a pair of underwear. "This is our shot, Coletta. I can't make mistakes on this one."

It takes me several beats to digest his plan. I have no valid arguments, other than a childish "I don't wanna," so I nod on my way out of the bathroom. "Okay. I'll stay with the sheriff."

Rome's shoulders lower as he exhales. I didn't realize he was this tensed about getting me to comply. "Thank you, tré-sur. Hopefully by this time next week, we can come back here and continue our honeymoon uninterrupted."

I quirk my brow at him. "Honeymoon?"

Rome smirks at me as he puts his shirt on. "Isn't that what humans do after they get married? A week of uninterrupted sex? This isn't much different than that."

My cheeks pink. "Yes. I didn't realize you were thinking such permanent thoughts. I mean, I know the mating bond has its own designs, but you really think of us as married?"

Rome moves out of the bathroom so he can kiss any uncertainty out of me. "If it were possible for vampires to marry, that's exactly what we would do."

My fingers twine in the collar of his shirt, holding him close because all too soon, I know he will be taken away.

12

MY SECRET GIRLFRIEND

It's so much easier to avoid my father when we are not under the same roof. The sheriff and I are doing our best to be extra polite because otherwise things will go south real quickly.

Rome dropped me at the salon when we got back into town, so I could take my car to the sheriff's house and park it in the garage.

Now I am cleaning my father's house, which isn't particularly dirty, but I can't sit still. After dusting everything in each room, I wipe down the baseboards, which haven't seen a dust rag in who knows how long. I take down all the light fixtures and wipe them out, so the dust particles don't dim the shine of the room.

After polishing the kitchen floor, I turn on the vacuum in the living room.

"Colette!" my father shouts, causing me to jump.

I turn off the machine, my hand moving over my heart. "You scared me!"

The sheriff holds up his hands. "Sorry. I called you a couple times, but you didn't hear me. I was going to turn in, but I'm guessing neither of us are going to get much sleep tonight. If I made a pot of tea, would you drink some?"

I consider his offer, muscling past the knee-jerk reaction to brush him off. "Decaf, sure."

"Of course." Instead of moving into the kitchen, he stands in the living room, staring at me with an inscrutable expression. "I called the officer who wrote up the report on the intruder. I figure asking you how you are wouldn't get me a straight answer. He told me you didn't get hurt. Is that accurate?"

I nod slowly. "I'm the one who fired the shots."

The sheriff rolls his shoulders back. "The officer told me he could tell you were my daughter, because they were perfect shots."

As far as compliments go, I guess that counts as one.

When I don't respond, the sheriff shoves his hands in the pockets of his jeans. "I looked up the owner of the cabin you were at. The identity is a dead end. The person doesn't exist." He purses his lips and exhales through his nose. "I don't know how to ask this, but do you have a fake identity that you use when you don't want to be found?"

I debate telling him about Rome but know that would

be a mistake. "If I did, I don't think I would admit to the scandal."

The corner of his mouth quirks. "Fair enough." He motions around his home. "You know, you don't have to clean. You can sit down and relax."

I shake my head. "Not sure that's possible, at this point. After shooting and killing a man, sleep isn't my most natural inclination."

He quirks an eyebrow at me. "This is the first person you've killed, right?"

I want to laugh at the question but go with a non-answer instead. "If I did kill before, I don't think I would admit to that scandal, either."

He runs his hand over his face. "You're too much like me, Coco. Don't want to talk about the important things."

I shrug. "Apple, tree and all that, I guess." I unplug the vacuum and wind the cord. "I'm really fine. Just over-thinking everything." I take a leap and open up the smallest amount. "I don't like the idea of my home not being safe to return to."

The sheriff watches me, no doubt shocked that I have divulged this obvious fact about myself. "You can always stay here. For as long as you like, Coco."

I nod. "Thanks. I still can't get over the fact that you are the only person who knew where I was, and I was still attacked. I know you didn't tell anyone. It's just weird. Makes me extra jumpy."

"Understandable. I really didn't tell anyone. I've been racking my brain about that, too. The only thing I can think is that someone put a bug on your phone. But I pried it open in the kitchen just now, and I couldn't find anything."

I narrow my eyes at my father, though I am not particularly angry about his confession. "What a fabulous invasion of my privacy."

"I didn't want to worry you, in case there might have been private conversations on that phone you didn't want anyone to overhear." It seems like he is hinting at something, but I can't figure out what. He is still under the impression that Rome and I are having a fake relationship for the public only. He couldn't possibly suspect we are real.

I want to call Rome, but this is not the time. He needs to be focused on getting Frank's son to safety and closing down any traces of halluci-blend, now that he is found the root of the problem.

"Are you hungry?" I ask my father, even though it's past dinner time. The sun is just about set, and if memory serves, my father eats dinner early, like an old man should. "I can order us something."

The corner of his mouth lifts. "Sure. Now that I've gone off my macro diet, I've had a hankering for chicken fried rice. And ribs. And macaroni and cheese—the gooey kind with enough dairy to stop a runner's heart."

I chuckle at his appetite, but I catch the true sadness behind it. "You're really throwing in the towel, are you?"

He holds my gaze. "If you don't have to talk about shooting a man, then I don't have to talk about doctor stuff. I've made my decision, and I'm sticking to it. I don't want to fight anymore. I've given chemo the old college try, and here I am."

I want to tell him to try it with me holding his hand, but even as I think it, I can't conjure up a believable image.

"Okay. Before I order all the food in the world, is there anything I should know? Because you look normal. Tired, but normal."

He turns his head to the side to avoid looking at me. "That tired look is going to get worse. I sleep most of the time, actually. Last week, we didn't get around to me telling you, but I retired from the force. I don't have the energy to move around like I need to. I sleep most of the day, putz around in the evening, and then sleep the night through. I think that's the way things are going to play out for a while." He rubs the nape of his neck. "Incontinence is no picnic. That's all I'll say about that."

My mouth screws to the side. "What does Declan say?"

At this, he fixes me with a pointed stare. "Maybe you should ask him yourself. You can be mad at me all you want, but you need to let your brother off the hook for keeping my secret. I put him in a tough position, yet you're intent on hanging him for it."

It's my turn to look away. "I'll call him when I'm ready. It still stings."

My father straightens. "Fair enough." He slaps his hands together. "I think I'm behind on that Bloody Ninja Blood-Blood movie series you and Declan always talk about. Let's watch that while we eat."

I snicker at his butchering of the title. "You mean Blood Ninja Disco?"

"Sure. Whatever it's called. I'll make a phone call while you order the food. Sound good?"

I smirk because it does sound good. It's surreal, spending a lazy evening with my dad. Ordering too much food and watching the best bad movies in the world. I can't believe it's taken us this long to get here. "That sounds perfect."

I order everything he requested, plus a dessert because I don't want to skimp on a movie night with my father. I always wanted to do something like this. Something normal.

By the time the food comes, I am starved for greasy food and a great movie. The two of us change into pajama pants like children readying for a slumber party.

When the doorbell rings, I scamper to answer the door, but my father reminds me I'm not to do that. "I've got it," he assures me. Before he opens the door, he fixes me with a meaningful look. "This is my night with my best girl. We're going to do this right."

"With fried rice?" I joke.

When he pulls open the door, I am surprised to find Rachel on my porch with a pleasant smile on her face. "Hi-ya, Boss. Hello, Sheriff."

My head tilts to the side as I smile at the manager of my salon. "Rachel? What a nice surprise." I usher her in and hug her. "Is something wrong with the salon?" My nose crinkles. "Wait, how did you know I was here?"

Rachel jerks her thumb to the sheriff. "A certain someone invited me over for a movie night."

I blink up at my father, confused at the addition to our plans.

The sheriff is wearing nice pajamas, which should have been a clue that he was still expecting company. "I don't want us to have secrets anymore, Coco. I invited Rachel over here because I don't want you to have to keep her from me."

The more he talks, the less sense he makes. "Huh? I've never kept you from Rachel. I didn't even know you cared about meeting her. You've met. She manages the salon."

The sheriff fixes me with a wry expression. "Yes, I've met her as your branch manager, but there's no need to hide your relationship from me. After I welcomed in Declan's fella, I should think it obvious that I'm not going to be a problem when it comes to you being in a relationship with another woman. Love is love, and all that. I don't want you hiding someone important from me."

My jaw drops as Rachel holds her hand over her mouth to stifle a laugh. "What?" she squeaks. "Oh, that's so sweet! What a supportive dad."

I massage my temples. "This is a nightmare."

Rachel shakes my father's hand. "I'm actually seeing someone who is definitely not your daughter."

The sheriff frowns at the two of us. "But you're seeing someone, Coco. You got all squirrely, thinking I wouldn't approve. You had candles lit when I stopped over without calling first. Then when you were at the cabin, you said 'we'. You were together up there, right?"

Rachel shakes her head. "I was closing down the salon tonight." She turns toward me. "Everything okay, Boss?"

"Other than this? Yeah, everything's fine."

The sheriff's thick brows push together, his irritation flaring. "Now, look here. I know you're seeing someone. If it's not Rachel, then who? I'm not playing around, Coco. This kind of thing matters. I'm not going to be around long. I'd like to know what it looks like to see my daughter happy with a partner."

I pinch the bridge of my nose. "Rachel, could I be rude and tell you I need time with my father to work this out?"

Rachel cannot stop giggling. "Not a problem. See you later, Colette."

When the door shuts behind her, I lean against it, closing my eyes and trying to think of how I can get out of this, other than stonewalling my father and shutting down our almost perfect movie night.

"Is there a way we can pretend that didn't happen?" I ask him.

The bags under his eyes are that much more visible now. "Not really. I'm serious, Coco. I want to know you're in good hands. I want to know you're going to have a good life."

"Meeting my boyfriend might not assure you of all that."

His jaw tightens. "I still want to know."

I hang my head. "Fine. You might want to sit down for this. If the cancer hasn't taken you down, a heart attack might."

The two of us sit down on the couch in the newly cleaned living room, facing each other while we brace ourselves for the truth that is about to hit the air and wreck our one chance at trust.

13

TELLING THE SHERIFF THE TRUTH

I have envisioned telling my father about Rome. Over and over, I've rehearsed the script, but the results are always the same. He yells at me until his face turns red, and then he storms to his patrol car to take his rage out on my boyfriend.

"Are you allowed to drink in your condition?" I ask my father, wanting to give myself every advantage.

"I can do whatever I want because the consequence is already determined. But I don't need a shot of whiskey to listen to my daughter tell me about her dating life." He presses his lips together, no doubt frustrated with us both. "We can do this. Really, Coco. I believe we can talk about normal things in our lives. I promise not to overreact. Did you see how okay with everything I was when I met Declan's boyfriend?" He motions to himself. "Cool as a cucumber."

"I'm going to remind you that you said that when you hit the ceiling." We are on opposite ends of the couch in the living room, facing each other with determination schooling our expressions. "I don't know how to start this," I admit.

"I can be patient, so long as you come clean tonight. I'm serious, Coco. I know I don't deserve a peek into your life, but I'm asking you sincerely to let me in. My dying wish."

I glower at him. "That's a low blow."

My father chuckles. "I can fake a cough if that sweetens the pity pot."

I swallow hard. "You're going to be mad."

He shrugs. "I've been mad before."

"You won't like him."

"Ha!" the sheriff barks, making me jump in my seat. "You're halfway there. You just told me it was a him. We're getting somewhere."

I snort a laugh because even that feels like an overshare.

Rome's advice to me while he was in the shower after the shootout reminds me that one day, I might wish things could have been different between my father and myself. I might want to have tried to have this conversation.

If I can't be brave for my father, then perhaps I can be brave for my future self, who no doubt will have enough cards stacked against her.

I wet my lower lip, gathering my gumption to find the

thread of where this whole affair started. "Remember way back when Nino-bear broke into my salon before it opened and trashed the place?"

"I remember."

"Rome stopped by after that to make amends. We had a good talk, and started talking more often."

The sheriff doesn't react at all, other than a nod, which tells me he isn't going to get there on his own. I have to actually spell it all out. "Rome introduced you to someone he trusts? That's nice. He has good instincts. Why would I be mad about that?"

I am flustered, so my mind skips several important details on its way to my confession. "Orlando was worried about my safety, so he started watching the salon. Watching me. Keeping tabs on any threats. We started to become friends. Hung out a few times. It was nice." I clear my throat, wishing for a natural disaster to come along and steal the words from me so I don't have to say them. "Do you know much about vampire mating?"

The sheriff blinks at me. "I mean, a little. It doesn't happen all that often, though, so most of what I think I know could be wrong." He leans forward with intrigue lightening his features. "Did Orlando mate with some-one?" He shakes his head at the mysteries of the world. "I can't even picture him on a date. I guess stranger things have happened, though I can't think of any off-hand. That's amazing. Good for him." Then my father jabs his finger in my direction. "But I'm not asking about Orlando's dating life; I'm asking about yours."

I chew on my lower lip, knowing I'm telling this all wrong. "Um, yes he sort of did mate with someone, but it's a little more complicated than that. See, there was an incident." I wave my hand to clear the air. "It doesn't matter what. There was an incident that left me in a bad way. I couldn't hold onto my body heat. Food tasted weird. I couldn't calm down to sleep. I was off and I couldn't figure out why. Orlando was watching my house at the time, so he tried a little experiment. He put a few drops of his blood into my tea."

Whatever my father expected me to say, that was certainly not it. He leans back, his voice grave. "Orlando did what?"

"It was a theory, and it turned out to be spot on. I felt much better, and continued to get better. Not just the cold and food tasting weird, but my tremors went away. So long as I drink a little of Orlando's blood every day, all the downsides of being a Deadblood go away."

My father's hand spreads over his gaping mouth. He blinks at me, emotion welling in his eyes. "Are you serious? Did you tell your doctor? What does Declan say about this? Who would have thought vampire blood would do something so miraculous? That's incredible, Coco! You're really better?"

I cast him a wan smile as I nod. "As far as I can tell, yes.

I still have to take my meds, but the combo of pills with Orlando's blood seems to be the thing my body needs. The catch is that me drinking Orlando's blood the way I did bonded me to him. It's the vampire mating bond. So I can feel his more potent mood swings. I can tell when he's physically hurt. I know what he needs without him telling me. It's like this psychic connection. I can't read his mind or anything, but I know how to be good to him." I hold up my hands. "It's nothing romantic, but it's a tight bond, for sure. He's one of my best friends now."

The sheriff's eyes are round as he lets loose an incredulous laugh. "Well, that's a twist I didn't see coming. So all this time, you've been hanging around with Orlando because he accidentally mated with you?" He laughs harder. "For a second—I know this is crazy—but I thought you were going to tell me that you and Orlando are dating! Can you imagine?" His laughter gains volume as he claps his hands. "Oh, I'm sorry. I don't know what's wrong with me. This is all great news, Coco. I wish you would have told me sooner. You're really doing better? The shakes are truly gone?"

I grimace because his laughter is about to disappear.

"Hold onto what's left of your hair, Sheriff. There's more." I take in a deep breath, knowing this is about to get much worse before it has a chance at getting better. "The thing is, when Rome came to the salon back when Nico trashed it, we realized how much we have in common. We got to talking. Then we got to texting. Then we had a few phone calls." I swallow hard. "Then we started dating in secret."

My father's joy dies on his lips. His movements still. I'm not sure he is daring to breathe.

I rush through my story. "The reason why my body started freaking out, making me cold and turning food bad in my mouth was because Rome and I were kissing, and something happened. I heard a gong or a pop or something, and he got spooked and ran. Well, it turns out, that kiss set off nature trying to mate us together, even though he's a vampire and I am clearly not. When he ran out, it left my body in sort of a state of crisis. Orlando guessed at what was happening. He figured his blood is genetically similar enough to Rome's that the bond could complete itself if I drank some of his blood." My throat dries. "But the bond took a left turn and fused me to Orlando. So even though we're not romantically involved, I know him. I understand Orlando, and he understands me."

My father presses three fingers to his lips. Still no sound comes out. I'm not sure if he is comprehending anything I am saying now, but I continue on, if only to have crossed this story as completed off my list of conversations to have.

"When Rome stopped freaking out and came back, we

took our time getting back together. It's complicated, for all the obvious reasons." My voice drops in volume, warning me that I am on the edge of hitting my limit with open communication. "When you dropped that bomb of your diagnosis on my head at family dinner, I wanted to run away. So Rome took me to a cabin he owns under a false name, and we holed up there for... however long I've been gone. We..." I cannot say "had sex" in front of my father, so I opt for a more demure, "We made things official in the cabin, and the bond took another twist. Apparently, humans *can* mate with a vampire." I pause, gnawing on my lower lip. "In fact, we can mate with multiple vampires." I fiddle with the hem of my tank top, surprised the ground hasn't cracked open and swallowed me whole. "Orlando's blood keeps my genetics from taking over. Rome's blood... It's still new to me, but so far it seems that I heal quicker, like a vampire might. I scraped my knee in the middle of the night in the cabin, but by morning it was scabbed over, like it had a week to heal."

My father is gob smacked, staring at me as if I am an alien come down from my spaceship to ask him how humanity has survived this long with our heads up our butts when it comes to most issues. "You... You're dating Rome. Rome Valentino. Your secret boyfriend is Rome Valentino."

I take my time answering, but a nod is the most I can offer. I think I used up the last of my words getting us here.

"You're mated (which isn't even possible for humans) to two vampires." My father rubs his forehead. "Two vampires who are a decade older than you."

Another nod. "I know my life is weird, but it's the happiest I've ever been. I don't expect you to approve or understand, but you wanted the truth, so there it is."

"It's not possible," he argues. "Mating is rare, and only between two vampires. Not two vampires and a human."

"To be fair, Orlando and Rome aren't mated. They're both bonded to me."

Not like that's the point to focus on.

"It's impossible," the sheriff rules.

"Actually, it's improbable because vampires and humans have never dated before. For all we know, it's always been possible; we were all just too bigoted to realize it."

The sheriff shakes his head. "Rome isn't fit to be anyone's boyfriend. He's married to Mayfield, Coco. This is..." He stands, anger flaring his nostrils. "This is unthinkable! I'm just glad I'm the only one who knows."

"Well..." I grimace. I decide to throw Declan under the bus because I am still a little mad at him. "Declan knows, too. And Lucas. We double dated that night you met Lucas at the theater."

The sheriff closes his eyes. "Tell me you're lying. Tell me you're trying to give me a heart attack, so I don't die of cancer."

I blanche, knowing this was never going to go over well. At least the sheriff isn't yelling.

Scratch that.

My father's voice thunders through the living room. "He's a vampire, Colette! And he's the head of the Valentino family. He is so much older than you! No! You couldn't possibly want to date Rome."

I shrug, going for broke because I have already pushed us both to the edge. "Actually, I'm in love with Rome. Once this business in the West End is cleared up and he stops the halluci-blend from coming into the city, we're going away from Mayfield so we can be together."

My father holds his hands over his ears, childishly trying to shut out my words. "No! No, you're doing nothing of the sort. I've had it with this, young lady. It's not happening. End it now. Right now. No daughter of mine is going to end up with a vampire."

The doorbell rings, so I move to collect the takeout, knowing that whatever fantasies I entertained of being close with my father were dreams that will never come true.

I tried. At least after the sheriff is gone, I will be able to be honest with myself about that.

But when I open the door, it's not the delivery person with our food. Orlando is carrying a little boy of maybe ten years old. "I need to stash them here," he tells me in lieu of a greeting. "No one will think to breech the sheriff's house."

I stand aside, numb to almost every upset.

"Is it true?" the sheriff asks Orlando.

Even though Orlando can only guess at what we've been discussing, he pales as he steps into the house. "I need to put the boy somewhere. I called Declan to come and give him a look. He's alive, but he's in bad shape. I don't know much about kids, but this isn't how I'd want mine to be treated."

I motion to the hallway, offering Orlando one of the bedrooms there. "Good that you got him out. We'll watch him."

But whatever other assurances I want to give Orlando are cut short when Rome enters into the house next.

"You!" my father roars. Then he storms to the entrance and punches my boyfriend square across the face.

Time seems to still while my mind struggles to made sense of the scene playing out before my eyes.

No part of me can handle what I am witnessing. After pouring my heart out about the relationships that have changed my world, my body and my heart, my father reacted in the way that is most predictable.

My hands cover my mouth to keep my scream from piercing the air. "You didn't... I didn't mean to..."

But none of my words offer the slightest bit of help.

Rome holds his cheek, his eyes wide, true hurt beaming out from him and aimed directly at my father. He doesn't speak or defend himself. In fact, I am fairly certain that if my father kept wailing on Rome, my boyfriend would take every blow and not raise a hand to stop the assault.

The sheriff raises his fist to do exactly that, but my heart can't take it. "No!" I race to the two, sliding in front of Rome just as my father's fist flings out with no sense of control or humanity.

I don't even have time to brace myself as my father's fist connects with my face. Though he is in his sixties, his punch lacks nothing, drawing from his years of service on the force.

My mind blanks as inexpressible heartbreak shatters what is left of my hope.

I had hope, however feeble. When I opened up and shared about my personal life, I had hope that the sheriff would hear it. I wasn't so naïve that I thought he would be happy for me, but my hope was that he could look at my life and be relieved that he knows me. That we can talk about things we disagree on, even when they are hard.

The horror that rings through my body matches the terror on my father's face. Neither of us saw this coming.

My thoughts begin to swirl to incoherence, my mouth uttering something unintelligible.

Before I can work out proper speech, my vision blurs,

letting me know that while my heart might have been prepared to take a blow for the man I love, my body cannot withstand a direct hit to my head.

The atmosphere dims as my knees go out from under me.

14

CANNOT SAVE MYSELF

When I awake, Rome's panicked expression fills my vision. I get the feeling I was only out for half a minute or so, but that small separation of me from my faculties has me spooked as the world comes back to me in fits and starts.

"Tré-sur, look at me. Tell me we haven't lost each other."

His lip is split, but there is nothing in his face that indicates he cares about his own injury as he holds me on the floor of my father's home beside the front door, spread across his lap. His focus is solely on me.

My hand reaches up to grab his collar, but my grip is weak.

He exhales, though his distress is far from over. "You're awake. I'm here. I'm right here." We sit together a few yards away from my father, though he is still in full view of us.

Now that I am awake, it is clear to me that beneath the relief, Rome's rage is palpable. I can feel it radiating out into the house. His hand guides my chin away from my father, who is frozen in stunned silence.

Though he is furious, Rome's voice has a deadly calm to it. His eyes lock in on mine with no trace of weakness anywhere on his person. His chest is broad, and displeasure is so grand that I shrink under the weight of it. "We will agree on one thing right now. All attacks aimed my way are for me to deal with, not you."

I will never agree to that, and he knows it. We are the same wild animal, bred to protect the ones we love.

Though Rome was just punched in the face, too, he is solely attentive to me. He holds a finger up, telling me to focus on it so he can check my eyes are moving how they should.

"Forgive me for this." He pulls out his phone and calls the one person who will crumble any walls I have carefully put in place. "Declan, I need you to come to your father's house. Quicker, then. The sheriff punched your sister in the side of her head. She blacked out, but she's awake now. You've got your medical bag? Good. You know more about this stuff than I do."

I lie in his arms in stunned silence, unsure how I didn't see this coming. Why did I tell my father anything about me? This isn't how I want my life to go, yet here I am.

My regrets line up, drowning out Rome's voice as they present themselves to me one by one.

My thoughts are mushy. Each time I cling to a musing, it blurs and becomes hard to hold onto. Rome is talking to me now while Orlando beelines to his side, apprising himself of the situation at hand.

Orlando never shows fear, but when he touches my temple with a handkerchief, he pulls his hand away to show me crimson on the cloth.

My father must've clocked me with his ringed hand. Not many men have diamonds on their wedding bands, and even fewer men still wear theirs decades after their wife passed, but my father is a romantic, I guess.

My mother would be furious if she knew her family had devolved to this.

I want to tell Rome and Orlando not to go near my blood, but I can't make my mouth move in any controlled rhythm to work out the words.

Orlando rushes to the kitchen, coming back with a wet rag for the side of my head. Orlando positions his body between myself and my father, who is still frozen between the living room and the front door, eyes wide with shock.

"It's okay," Orlando tells me, which I think might be the first lie he's ever said to me.

I open my mouth to tell him as much, but when I speak, my words come out jumbled and not what I mean for them to be. I try to clear my throat, but I can't manage that, either. I try again, but my words are incoherent, even to my own ears.

Rome swears as he shouts into the phone for Declan to hurry.

I want to tell the two of them to give my blood a wide berth. They are cleaning up my temple carefully, but the risk worries me because I love them both so much.

But my words fail me. It's not even sentences that come out, but a string of random syllables that sound nothing like what I mean to say.

Orlando kneels beside us, a wet rag pressed to my temple. "We can't leave the child here. Not if Elias is throwing punches. The kid's been through enough."

Rome doesn't seem to be digesting Orlando's concern. His eyes stay locked in on mine for minutes on end.

"You have to let me try, Rome," Orlando tells him.

I'm only catching bits and pieces of their exchange, barely understanding why Rome finally nods and angles my body from his.

Orlando pinches my cheeks to pop my mouth open after tearing at his own wrist with his fang. "Drink as much as you can," he instructs. "Until Declan gets here, it's our best shot at helping you."

My mouth isn't working how I want it to, but after a few drips drizzle down my throat, my swallow reflex kicks in. The honeyed warmth slides over my tongue as I drink the crimson and hope for the best. Orlando's blood has kept the effects of my genetics from taking my body down a grim path; it's worth a shot to hope that an extra helping of his blood might counteract whatever damage is setting in, taking my language from me.

I can't let this happen; I've worked too hard to recover and move on with my life.

The flavor of Orlando is incredible, and pushes my most pressing worries to the back of my mind. The blood Orlando gives me in the flask is delicious, but fresh from his wrist?

I could drink this by the bottle.

Orlando's free hand moves around to cup the back of my head, helping me angle my mouth just so. I want more of him, always more.

It's a long shot to guess that his blood which stops my genetics from taking over might also undo head trauma, but it's our only option.

I won't go back to having to rely on people to get around. I won't give up my freedoms now.

Orlando's breathing turns ragged. "We should see a change if my blood is the ticket," he tells Rome. "There's hardly any delay from her body relaxing itself once she has my blood."

Rome nods. "Let's see if it worked."

After Orlando pulls his wrist from my mouth, Rome cups the side of my face, turning my chin so I can stare up at him. "Talk to me, Coletta. Please. Tell me how foolish I am to be smitten with you. Cuss me out. Anything!"

I open my mouth, but the assurances I want to give Rome that I will always love him don't hit the air. "Ameena-moof-oo."

Rome's heartbreak hits the air. "No!" Then he glances at Orlando. "My blood. Maybe it's my blood she needs. Or both our blood together. I don't know!"

Orlando shrugs, because there are no bad ideas in brainstorming.

Rome's voice sounds on the edge of hysteria. "She told me that after we mated, she heals more quickly. She scraped her knee, but by morning, the mark was nearly gone. It's me. She needs me!"

Before I can tell Rome that I have no idea if his blood can heal something as dangerous as head trauma, Rome is already pressing his wrist to his fang, tearing open the flesh.

I don't like to see him bleeding. Any part of him that is hurt makes my insides tremble to stop his pain.

But I don't have the opportunity to tell him that. Rome's wrist presses to my lips, drenching my mouth with a steadier stream of blood. My throat constricts, welcoming his blood into my system.

My eyes roll back as pure pleasure coats my insides.

Orlando's worry feels far away, even as he shouts, "Is she having a seizure? What's happening? Is she fainting?"

But I can't care about the drama of the day. Not when Rome's blood is filling my belly.

Rome tastes like berries picked fresh from a sun-heated garden. The flavor mutates in sharpness, turning up the sweet notes and then the sour details of the berry.

More. When Rome pulls away his wrist, I cry out an incoherent plea for more.

Though I still can't make myself known, Rome understands me because we are the same monster. We were both fated to be the symbol that set off hate in the world around us. We are glorified as much as we are vilified. We care about the Mayfield with a burning passion because we know that if we don't save the last city where vampires are free, there is no hope for them—or for the humans who let their ignorance and hatred run the show.

"What's happening? Is it working?" The sheriff asks from his spot a few feet away.

Orlando turns with a snarl. "She is no longer your concern."

I drink from Rome because he is the only beautiful spot in my dimming world. I crave the taste of him, the flavor of comfort paired with possibility.

Something pops in my brain—a physical blip inside the right half of my cranium. It scares me because I don't know if this sensation is friend or foe. Is it breaking me more, or is it doing its best to fix me?

Rome's face goes in and out of my vision as it blurs and

then fights for focus. His lower lip quivers, then his upper lip curls. He goes from scared boy to angry man, and back again over and over until a numbing sensation takes me over, and I pass clean out.

I cannot save the world from itself.

In this moment, I cannot even save myself.

15

MIRACLE

Fear doesn't suit me. It never has. Even the times I was abducted and my blood drained over and over, fear wasn't the overwhelming emotion. It was there, sure, but my need for independence was stronger.

Always has been.

The minutes it takes for Rome's blood to move through my body and fix all unseen damage feels like an eternity. Every moment I cannot speak for myself is a horror no one should ever experience.

At least my eyes are open. I'm not sure how long I was passed out for, but in the time I was unconscious, Orlando broke out in a sweat and Rome has gone from scared to terrified.

Rome's tears dot my face as over and over he whispers, "Why isn't it working?"

I've never seen Rome cry before. Even as I feel pops and sizzles inside my brain, the larger focus is the sight of him showing raw emotion. I've seen him naked, vulnerable and needy, but this is a new facet of the man I will never stop loving. He sees me, even when there are parts of me that I think I have cleverly hidden. He is good to me, even when I am too busy to notice right away.

I lie in his arms, sprawled across his lap like a limp noodle. Aside from the definite terror over the state of my health, the most prevalent emotion that surfaces is the only thing that comes out of my mouth when I finally dare to try speaking again.

"I love you," I tell Rome. My words are clear, though weighted with emotion.

Rome throws his head back and wails like a man undone. He clutches me tighter to his chest from his spot beside the front door, guiding my face to the crook of his neck.

I do love him. I love him without limits, as I never thought I could do for any man. I love him enough to protect him and stand beside him while the world refuses to accept, evolve and love. If the world doesn't have enough kindness in it to welcome us, then we will manufacture our own love.

And it will be enough to keep our heads held high and our fingers woven together.

Orlando stands when Declan bursts in through the front door.

At this, my father finally snaps to attention, coming out of his stunned haze. "Declan, I..."

"Don't." Declan's command is firm as he drops his medic bag next to the spot where Rome is huddled on the floor with me still sprawled across his lap. My brother kneels beside us and opens his bag, taking a pen light and shining it in my face. "Your eyes aren't focusing all the way. Well, the right one is, but the left one isn't."

Almost as if his words remind my body that it still has work to do, a loud pop explodes in the left hemisphere of my brain. It is so powerful that I flinch, as if the sensation is audible.

"Rome, you have to loosen your grip. I need to test her reflexes, so I know what we're dealing with."

Rome shakes his head, though he doesn't appear to be belligerent, but more afraid. "I can't. I don't know why, but I can't. I can't let go. She's hurt, Declan. She took a punch aimed at me right in the head. If she's... If this..." He holds me tighter. "I can't let go."

Orlando seems to understand Rome's psychosis. He lowers himself with a grunt and sits across from Rome, crossing his legs so his knees touch his cousin's. "Give her to me. You know you can trust me with your life and with hers. She's bonded to me just as tightly. Let me hold her right here, where you can see everything. Not a thing happens without you right here."

Declan's nostrils flare. "This is dysfunctional. I need to size up the scope of the damage. Either you hand her over, or things can get physical. Right now, Rome."

Rome doesn't respond to Declan's threat, but to Orlando's offer of care. His arms tremble as his torso leans forward, handing my body off to Orlando, who doesn't move too suddenly or take me from Rome too quickly. As promised, Orlando keeps me right in Rome's eyeline.

"She said she loves me," Rome tells Declan.

My brother rolls his eyes. "I wouldn't start picking out China patterns just yet. No one's going to be thrilled to hear their head vampire has fallen in love."

Rome swipes the tears off his cheeks. "I'm telling you she spoke coherently, dumbass. A whole sentence."

Declan's jaw tightens. "Oh. Okay, that's good news."

"She has feeling and muscle control in her hands at least. She was gripping my shirt before she passed out."

"Also good." Declan has his serious paramedic face on as he pokes and prods, turning my limbs this way and that.

It's when he asks me if I know what day it is that my heart comes to the surface. "It's a week or two after our big fight." Tears dot my cheeks. "I'm sorry, Declan. I was mad you didn't tell me about the sheriff's cancer. You're my only family who loves me. I should have fought with you. I should have stayed and worked it out."

Declan drops his pen light and holds my hands, since the rest of me is in Orlando's grip. "Once you get better from this, you and I can fight it out for the next several decades. You got that? You don't take punches that are aimed at other people. Rome is a big boy; he can handle it."

I blink at my brother, unable to smile and nod along. "But I love him."

Declan closes his eyes. "I know. Let's hope it doesn't kill you."

I am alive.

I am alive and coherent.

16

BETTER AND WORSE

Relief spreads over me, though I know my body is not my own just yet. With Orlando's blood and Rome's in my system, I know I am on the way to recovery.

I can't believe I am smiling.

"I think we should buy Rome a pink shirt," I say to my brother. Though this is hardly the time for jokes, I can't help myself. "Do you think he would wear it?"

Declan chuckles. Our macabre humor in times of duress serves us well. "I think if he does, you need to parade him around town so everyone can appreciate their dapper vampire." He points to my legs. "But you'll need to be able to wear those ridiculous heels if you want to really draw people's eyes. Try to roll your ankle in a circle. Can you do that for me?"

I comply, continuing with the examination. The more

minutes that pass, the more alert my brain becomes. By the time Declan finishes, I am sitting up in Orlando's arms, his hand rubbing a slow circle across my back. My body isn't completely healed yet, but the scariest parts are not staring us in the face.

Declan runs his hand through his hair. "We're going to take a trip to the emergency room, just in case. We're going to have them do an MRI just as a precaution, but for now, it seems like the worst is behind us."

Famous last words, I want to say aloud, but I keep my grim outlook tucked inside.

Orlando's hand on my back doesn't feel unwelcome or foreign. On the contrary, he is part of me now. Perhaps he was even before we mated.

"It's our blood," Orlando explains to my brother. "Mine and Rome's this time."

Declan turns his head from one vampire to the other. "Do I want to know?"

Orlando doesn't give Declan the option to be in the dark. "We're both mated to your sister. She couldn't form sentences. But after Rome gave her his blood, her head cleared, and she could speak."

Declan's breath catches. His eyes lock in on mine, telling me with his gaze how worried he is, now that I have gone deeper into the muck. "You're in it now, Sis."

I chew on my lower lip, knowing that even if I could undo the bond I share with Rome and Orlando, I would not dare. I love them—in different ways, sure, but I wouldn't trade it for anything.

"Is she alright?" my father's voice rasps from behind Declan.

Orlando holds me tighter as Rome stands in time with Declan rising to his feet.

Rome stares down my father in a manner that causes my body to burrow further into Orlando's. "I thought my cousin made himself clear. She is not your concern anymore."

"It was an accident," the sheriff explains. "I would never aim for my own daughter. I meant to hit you, Rome, but she got in between us."

Declan slings his arm over Rome's shoulder and turns the sheriff around toward the back of the house. "Before I take your daughter to the ER, let's the three of us have a little chat in the backyard." He fakes a laugh. "Actually, no. I'll do the talking, and you'll do the nodding. Those are my favorite kinds of chats."

Orlando exhales the moment the three exit out the backdoor. He buries his face in my hair. "Is it safe to breathe yet? I swear, my heart was pounding harder through that whole ordeal than when we went into Fairfax's hideout and rescued the boy."

"I'm glad you're here," I offer in a quiet voice.

Orlando snorts. "I don't hear that often, but I'll take it." His free hand rubs slow circles across my back. "You scared me, Coco. I don't do scared."

"I don't do helpless, so I guess this is a day of firsts all the way around."

He tilts my body to lean more comfortably against his, inhaling the scent of my hair. "Mm."

We sit like that for minutes on end, relaxing in the gratitude that we survived danger when it was staring us in the face.

The solace is interrupted by the chime of Orlando's phone. "How's the job?" Orlando asks, cutting to the chase. After a few grunts, he sighs. "I'll be there in twenty."

When he ends the call, he makes no move to stand. Instead, he kisses the top of my head, letting his lips rest in my hair.

My hand rests over his heart because I know exactly where it beats. "Were there any hiccups with the rescue mission? And did you reach out to Frank yet to let him know you have his son?"

Orlando jerks his head toward the hallway. "Declan needs to give the boy a look when he comes back inside. That was Nico on the phone. He was supposed to call me when he cleaned out Fairfax's place. A decent amount of interrogating needs to be done to make sure this is the last stop in all of it. It's a big promotion day for Nico, so he's going to go the extra mile on this one. Everyone is accounted for except one person, who apparently escaped out the back. Nico needs my help breaking down one of the criminals. He's gone through three already and couldn't get them to give up the name of the person who escaped. Apparently that's the one who's been cooking the halluci-blend, so we need to track him down."

"You have to go?"

"Have to. Don't want to. But we're close to halluci-blend being a thing of the past, so I need to help Nico snap this off." He kisses my hair again. "I don't want to interrupt the guilt trip your brother is giving the sheriff, but I should go. You okay here with Declan and Rome?"

I angle my face up and kiss his prickly cheek. "More than okay. Go on."

"I hate leaving you the second you come back to us."

"It's fine. Can I watch over the boy?"

Orlando nods. "I was hoping you'd volunteer for that. The kid is passed out. They'd injected him with a sleeping drug when we got there to keep him from giving them up. If he sleeps until I bring his dad here, so much the better."

"Agreed."

Orlando moves me to sit on the floor as he rises to his feet. When I make to stand, he puts a stop to that daredevilish act. "Not so fast." He leans down and scoops me up.

It's just as well. I'm not actually sure if my legs are working just yet.

"My purse?" I request, motioning to where it rests in the living room. "I think my phone is in there. In case you need me after you leave."

Orlando snags up my purse and carries me to the guest bedroom, which used to be Fintan's room when we were kids. The lights are out and Orlando doesn't bother to turn them on. Still, I can see the little boy sleeping atop the mattress.

My heart instantly swells and shatters. "He's so small. His hand is bandaged."

"That's where they..." Orlando doesn't finish his sentence.

I know that is the hand where the criminals took off the boy's finger to mail it to his father to get Frank to comply.

Orlando pulls out the chair from the desk and helps me to sit down. He presses my purse into my grip. "I know you're packing in here. Keep this on you. Don't let anyone but Rome, Declan or myself take this boy out of this room."

I swoon for Orlando, though this is hardly the time for heartfelt moments. I reach up, and Orlando compensates by leaning over, his face nearing mine.

I don't think through my actions. Instead, I do as my heart instructs. My lips brush against Orlando's because I love him so much. "You trust my brother," I explain of my affection for him.

Orlando pecks my lips. "Watch the boy. I'll be back in a bit."

"Be safe," I tell him as he leaves the room.

He doesn't answer because his own safety has never been a concern of his.

But now that I love Orlando and Rome so much, I know I will not be able to rest until they are both home and unharmed.

FINTAN'S LIMP

When the front door opens, I expect Rome, Declan and my father have returned from their walk.

But when only one set of shoes moves through the house, I wonder if Declan left Rome and my father to duke out their differences.

I really hope Declan didn't leave them unsupervised. Nothing good can come from that.

I've been watching the little boy for twenty minutes, counting his breaths and making sure his chest is moving. I don't know his name, but I do know that he was not cared for. He is all skin and bones, his cheeks hollow and his skin dry and dirty.

Though I don't know him, I feel a kinship with this boy. We've both been taken and hidden away because humans wanted to control things that ought not be theirs to destroy.

I am not destroyed. I can only hope this boy will one day be able to say the same.

"Dad?" I hear Fintan call from the living room. "Declan?"

I get up out of my seat, setting my purse onto the floor before I move into the hallway. I'm not terribly steady on my feet, but I can walk without incident, thank goodness. "They're outside."

Fintan's brows raise at the sight of me, his hand dipping into his coat pocket. "Oh! Coco, I didn't know you were here. Your car isn't in the driveway."

My eldest brother is wearing old jeans and hasn't taken off his shoes or his winter coat yet. He looks like he didn't get much sleep. His brownish-blond hair is sticking up in the back and he's got a smear of dirt on his cheek.

I keep my footsteps quiet as I walk toward him. "Did the sheriff call you? That's why you're here? Or did Declan tell you what happened?"

Fintan looks winded, but he takes his hands out of his coat pocket and raises them to let me know he doesn't want to take sides in the family. "All I know is that I'm here. What happened?"

Man, I wish Fintan was the kind of brother I could confide in. What a different life that would have been for us both.

I chew on my lower lip, unsure how to talk to him about the small things, much less the big ones that terrify me.

So I chicken out and give him the headline. I don't have to show Fintan that today was damaging. "The sheriff and I got into it."

Fintan snorts. "What else is new?" He glances around the house. "Rome's car is here. Did he bring the kid?"

My nose crinkles. "Declan told you about that?"

Fintan nods, a hopeful look on his face. "Yeah. I wanted to come by and check on the little guy."

Man, Declan's a chatty one. I didn't realize he'd called Fintan at all, much less telling him about our secret houseguest.

When the backdoor opens and Declan comes inside, he looks as if he is traveling with his own personal storm cloud as his eyes fall on me. "Just so you know, your boyfriend is not a tool, but your father most certainly is."

I cast Declan a wry look. "Not exactly a surprise."

Fintan nods toward Declan. "Hey, man. Anything I can help with? I can drive the kid into the emergency room. Take one thing off your plate."

Declan frowns. "How did you know the kid was sleeping in the guest room? I thought no one was supposed to know. And it's a vampire kid. They're not going to treat him at a medical facility. You know that."

My nose scrunches. "Fintan told me you told him over the phone."

Declan raises his hands. "I didn't call him."

Fintan waves off my confusion. "Dad called me. Guest room?" He points down the hallway. "Dad made it sound like the kid was in bad shape, so I'll take him to see a doctor. I know a guy who owes me a favor. He'll look at the boy for us."

My mouth screws to the side. "Orlando said not to move him. Declan can give the boy a look until Orlando says it's safe to take him in." I lean my back to the wall. "I'll call Orlando and ask."

Fintan moves toward me, but his gait is off. He's limping.

This detail hits me over the head as other clues begin clicking into place.

His dirty clothes and disheveled demeanor are unlike anything he would normally tolerate in his appearance.

He knew the child was here when we didn't tell him. The sheriff wasn't out of Declan's sight out there. He would have heard if the sheriff called Fintan and told him about the kid. He wouldn't have been surprised to see Fintan.

My eldest brother said Declan told him to come over, but then switched to saying it was our father, when it couldn't have been, because the sheriff was with either Declan or me the entire time. We would have overheard.

The revolution has been one step ahead of us at every turn. Notes left on my salon and car doors were found most of the time by Fintan or his buddy.

My heart slams in my chest as my brain clears away the last of the cobwebs.

His buddy's name is Fairfax. Steven Fairfax supposedly found a threatening note taped to the front door of my salon. The note was meant to scare me out of town. It was supposed to get me out of Mayfield.

Why? Why would my brother want me out of Mayfield?

Fintan limps toward me, and the final clue reveals itself.

I shot the second person who broke into Rome's private cabin. I killed Fairfax, but I only shot the second intruder in the leg.

I try to remember which leg I nailed, and then match it against Fintan's limp.

I shot my brother when he was wearing a ski mask and a world of hate.

Another clue pops into my mind: when Declan said I had a boyfriend just now, Fintan didn't question it.

Because he knows. He saw us in the cabin, barely clothed. He could have come into the sheriff's home and saw the address of the cabin scribbled on the notepad on the fridge, and that's how he found us.

"Wait!" I shout without meaning to. So much for playing it cool. I force a smile up at Fintan as he approaches. "Let me bring the little guy out to you. Go bring your car around, Fintan. I don't think the boy should be exposed to the elements if he doesn't have to be."

Fintan pauses but then moves toward the front door. "Good idea."

"I'll find some blankets, too. Give me a few minutes. Warm up your car? I don't want the boy chilly."

Fintan nods. "Not a problem."

The moment the front door closes, I whisper to Declan, who still looks frustrated at having to deal with the sheriff. "Declan! Fintan is a revolutionary!"

This snaps Declan out of his grumping. "What?"

"I was away with Rome this past week, and someone found us. The only person I told where we were was the sheriff, who probably told Fintan! He and his buddy came to the cabin and broke in. I shot the guy in the left leg. Fintan is limping! Did you see it?"

Declan holds up his hands. "Wait, what? You shot someone?"

Actually, I shot someone and killed another someone, but I don't have the time for a full explanation right now. "Go outside and make sure Rome is safe. Fintan knows Rome is my boyfriend! If he's a revolutionary, he might have bullets dipped in my blood. Get Rome out of here!"

Declan's horror tugs at his features. "Do you hear your-self? Our brother isn't..."

"Go!" I warn him, and then race to the guest bedroom on wobbly legs. I dig through my purse and pull out my phone, calling Orlando because I don't know who else to turn to.

Orlando picks up on the second ring, because he's just that good. "Everything okay?"

My reply is breathless and without the proper prep or politeness. "Fintan is the one who tried to break into the cabin and kill us. He's here now, telling me he's going to take the boy to get medical help. Orlando, I'm telling you, Fintan is behind this! He's part of the revolution!" My gaze settles on the sleeping boy, and my heart clinches in my chest.

Orlando swears, and I hear the car's tires screeching as he makes an about-face to come back here as quick as he can. "On my way to you. Under no circumstances are you to let that boy out of your sight. You've got your gun?"

I swallow hard. "I don't know if I can shoot my brother."

"You won't have to if you can stall him until I get there. He can't leave the house with Frank's son. That boy is the only person who can identify his abductors."

"I'll stall him until you get here." But I know I can't let that happen. I cannot allow Orlando to intervene because

Fintan might be carrying bullets that are deadly to the vampires I love.

I'm going to have to settle this before Orlando gets here.

I end the call when Fintan's steps echo down the hall. There's a normal tread and then a thump, letting me know I was not being paranoid. His leg is messed up because of me.

When Fintan steps into the guest room, he smacks his hands together. "Alright, car's ready."

"Blankets," I croak.

Fintan taps his temple twice. "Right. Good call. I'll grab one from the hall closet."

I am no good at holding back my rage. I'm no good at any of this. Though Fintan has never been my favorite person, I didn't think he was an actual villain capable of real horrors.

Fintan abducted Frank's son. After all our family has been through, Fintan stole a child from his father.

I keep my eyes on the boy's chest, watching him breathe. I let the movement of his ribcage settle my soul as much as it is able. I sit in the chair where Orlando left me, willing tranquility to steady my hands as I reach into my purse.

"This blanket should be good," Fintan says as he moves toward me from the hall closet toward the guest bedroom.

When Fintan steps into the room, his focus is on the

boy. I pull out my gun as calmly as I can while he makes his way to the bed.

Without warning and without hesitation, I take aim and fire, making sure Fintan doesn't lay a hand on the boy ever again.

18

THE DEBT OF THE REVOLUTION

Fintan's scream fills my father's house, but I feel nothing. Frank's son is still passed out atop the comforter on the guest bed. The drugs he was given spare him from the sight of my brother writhing on the floor, clutching his knee.

"Why? Why did you... Ah!"

The sound of the gunfire brings the sheriff, Rome and Declan inside. The three tear through the house to get to me. When they pile into the room, weapons drawn, they all start shouting at once.

I have no desire to explain myself. Not until I have all the answers I need.

I keep my pistol trained on Fintan as he holds his thigh, his teeth gritted together. "Anything you want to tell me, Finny?" I ask him, invoking the sacred use of the childhood nickname I used to call him, back when I was foolish enough to adore my eldest brother.

"You shot me!"

My voice is eerily calm. I feel as if I have left my body entirely, and some cold, cruel force of nature has taken over. "Twice. I shot you twice. Once in the knee just now, and once at the cabin when you tried to kill Rome and me."

The three men standing over Fintan whip their heads from me to him, suddenly mute as they realize there is more to this than they could possibly have guessed.

Declan covers his mouth with his hand. "Fintan, is that true?"

The sheriff closes his eyes. "Fintan was in the house with me when you gave me your address, Coco." He lowers his chin. "Tell me you didn't hunt down your own sister, Fintan."

Declan is incapable of being near an ailment and not treating it. He drops to his knees and winds the blanket Fintan was bringing into the room around the flesh wound.

Fintan's blood blooms over his shin, staining the carpet. "She's crazy! She's got a head injury. She doesn't know what she's saying! Get the gun away from her!"

The temptation to shoot Fintan again is strong, but I need a confession.

I need to know why.

I shake my head at him, my gun still trained on his writhing form. "Tell Rome who Steven Fairfax is."

Rome's nostrils flare. "Yes, tell me about the man who broke into my cabin."

Declan's brows pucker. "Your employee? Fintan, Steven broke into Rome's cabin? *You* broke into Rome's cabin? Why?"

Fintan throws his head back. "You're a medic, Declan! Help me!"

Declan removes the blanket from Fintan's knee, his mouth firm with displeasure. Then he reaches over and presses his thumb to the wound, drawing a scream from Fintan that makes my father flinch. "Why did you break into Rome's cabin?"

Fintan breathes heavily through his clenched jaw. "Why? Because she was going to disappear! I need the money, Declan. I'm in over my head."

Declan's brows knit together. "Coco owes you money? I don't understand."

I balk at the insinuation.

When Fintan clams up, Declan presses on the wound again. "Her blood is worth a lot! I needed to take her so I could sell her blood. It's the only way I could pay off my debts, now that Rome's cracked down on halluci-blend in the West End."

It takes a lot to shock me at this point, but that sure does it.

Rome finds his voice before I can form words. "You're the one who abducted Frank's son? *You* forced Frank to bring halluci-blend into the West End?" His eyes are wide as he covers his mouth. "You would know how, wouldn't you. When Dad had me cooking up halluci-mend in the basement, you were right there. You know how to make it properly. I guess you figured out how to bastardize it."

I have so many memories of Fintan and Rome talking together in the basement while Nino-bear and I were with Mama Valentino in the kitchen. They would stay down there for hours. I knew Rome was making halluci-mend, but it never dawned on me that Fintan was there the entire time, watching and learning. My brother was taking notes to birth his own drug empire someday.

Fintan grips Declan's arm, his bloody hand smearing crimson on Declan's wrist. "I didn't want it to go this far! I wasn't going to kill Coco. I swear, Declan! I was only going to hide her away for a while and take her blood. I didn't mean for her to get hurt the last time! I told them not to get rough with her! Steven knew the rules. The guys I worked with before didn't."

Bile rises in my throat.

It can't be true. It just can't. My brother didn't sell my blood for a profit. That's barbaric. It's unthinkable. It's an act of war.

Then again...

The sheriff covers his mouth with his hand. "No. I don't

believe it. You wouldn't try to sell your sister for cash."

My protest comes out hollow. "But he sold me for dates. Every guy Fintan set me up with paid him for the privilege of an ice-cold blind date with me."

Declan pales, his voice grave. "What?"

My father whimpers. "Fintan, I... All this time, it was you?" My head swims as the new horrors threaten to be too much for me to digest.

As much as I am able, I keep myself on my feet. I lower my gun, so I don't accidentally shoot Declan.

Fintan grips Declan harder as spittle flings out from his lips. "She's sleeping with him! Ah!" He throws his head back as pain rocks him off his balance. "When Fairfax and I got to the cabin, we saw them... together! It was supposed to be an act for the press to increase tolerance or whatever, but it's not an act, Declan! It's real!" He whispers, though not because he cares about my privacy. It's more like he can't stand the sound of the words hitting the air. "Our sister is sleeping with a vampire."

Declan's lower lip quivers. "I know. I know and I don't care. Fintan, what you've done... You abducted Coco? All those years ago, it was you? You're the reason she couldn't take care of herself? You're the reason she was sent away? You're the reason vampires have died?" His eyes close. "You abducted this little boy?"

"I had no other choice! I was going to lose my businesses, Declan! I've already had to take a loan out on the restaurant." Fintan tries to sit all the way up, but Declan presses on his bullet wound again to keep him on the floor.

Through Fintan's howling, I can hear Declan's heartbreak. "It's over now, Fintan. And in the end, you still lost your businesses."

My father lowers his head. "Fintan, all this time, it was you?"

Fintan whines his pain. "We could have been loaded if Coco would have donated her blood to the revolution."

While I am speechless, Declan is incredulous. "Mom left us each a sizeable trust. You *are* loaded!"

Fintan breathes through gritted teeth. "The loan business. It's not... I went through the money, okay? My trust is gone. I had a plan, Declan! All I needed was Coco's blood, and all my debts would be wiped clean."

I shake my head, finally piecing words together. "No. No, you wanted me to move back to Lonmure. You've been trying to get me out of Mayfield."

Fintan's shout is mingled with agony. "Because the people I owe money to didn't care how I got it! With you gone, I had a chance they wouldn't see your blood as an asset."

The sheriff leans against the far wall, his heart palpably broken. "Oh, Son. I am blind. I didn't realize how lost you are." He turns his head to me, looking completely devastated and far older than his years. "I'll take care of it, sweetheart. No one's going to come for you ever again."

The sheriff takes out his cell phone and calls the precinct, speaking in clipped tones while he requests a squad car and two paramedics to come to the house.

I can't move. I'm not sure I'm breathing. If I am, then my body is a fighter, because I can barely stand under the weight of my brother's betrayal.

All this time, it was Fintan.

Rome slides to my side, his hands only slightly steadier than mine as he removes my gun from my grip. He stands in between me and my brothers as he puts the safety on, blocking my view of Fintan.

When my gaze meets Rome's, I have nothing but heartbreak to offer him. I am a mere shell, horrified and gob smacked that this is how my family is going to crumble. "Fintan, he..."

"I know," Rome says in a low voice. He pockets my gun and then moves one of his arms behind my back. He sweeps my legs out from under me with his other arm. "I'm taking her to the living room. Declan, you got this?"

"Yeah. Fintan's unarmed now. The police are on their way."

Rome carries me to the living room and sits me on the couch while I wallow in my shock.

I thought I understood the shadowy threat that was the revolution. But as Rome holds my hand on my father's couch, I realize that the life I thought I understood was never as it seemed.

19

FATHER AND SON

Rome sits with me while the police come and do what they are trained to do. They're supposed to take away the criminal who is responsible for ruining countless lives. I had no idea one man could possess enough hatred in his soul to not only abduct a child and his own sister, but also to try and take down an entire people—by both deadly drugs and by a lethal weapon Fintan stole from my veins.

As angry as I probably still am at my father, pity softens the hardened edges of my heart. "Take him into the backyard," I whisper to Rome. "My father shouldn't have to see his son taken away in handcuffs."

"Whatever you need." Though Rome is no doubt just as affected at having his anonymous bad guy unmasked, he has been by my side this entire time. He even held my hand while I gave my statement to the police.

Orlando's call to Frank brought the broken dad to his son. Frank has been wailing loudly from the guest bedroom for a good five minutes while Orlando guards the hallway, so no one tears the two apart ever again.

Fintan is handcuffed to the gurney after the police take multiple statements, all leading them to the conclusion that Fintan's new residence will be prison, probably for the rest of his life.

"Dad!" Fintan shouts, breaking my heart with his desperation. "Dad, don't let them take me!"

My grief is heavy, keeping me rooted to the couch long after my brother is taken away. I would think Fintan's absence would breathe new life into my lungs, but I am still shattered without hope of anything being good ever again.

Not even when Rome ushers my father back into the house do I feel better. Rome sits quietly at my side, pressing a kiss to my temple. I will myself to embrace his warmth, but I feel nothing. I am hollow inside without a trace of optimism.

"I'm here," Rome assures me.

"I'm not," I admit. "I don't know where I want to be, but it's not here."

Rome nods once. "I'll take you away after we get this all settled."

It's a beautiful promise, and now that the culprit behind all the nefarious acts is going to be behind bars, there actually might be a chance for us to have a better life.

But I can't think that far ahead yet. I'm barely upright from the grief that is still ricocheting through me, even as Rome holds my hand.

When the second ambulance comes, there is a scuffle that reaches my ears, pulling me out of my shock for the moment.

"You know we can't treat the boy, Sheriff. He's a vampire child."

Declan still has our brother's blood on his hands as he inserts himself into the argument, putting his foot down. "I will treat the boy. I just need supplies." He tugs out his ID from the hospital, but still the medics are not convinced.

"We aren't trained for vampire emergencies," one of them protests.

It's a weak policy crutch the medical profession has always leaned on. The medical schools don't educate them on how to take care of vampires, so they feel little guilt on passing the blame to the educators, instead of taking it upon themselves to cross boundaries and learn of their own volition.

"I am," Declan tells them. "This boy needs help now. Start an IV and get out of my way. You can tell your boss I held you at gunpoint, if you like. I don't care. But one way or another, that boy is getting medical help."

"He'll heal on his own," the second medic argues.

"Their kind heal faster than we do. They don't need medical attention."

Declan's chest puffs. "We can do this the easy way or the hard way. That boy will not be abandoned when he's in need of help. Vampire or human doesn't matter. He's a child."

After a few more back and forths, and a promise from me that I will speak to their supervisor and let her know that they are letting Declan on their ambulance as a favor to the Last Deadblood, they finally agree.

Declan stands near me as the paramedics take their time moving the little boy out of the bedroom. My brother's arms are crossed over his chest as he wears a hard look on his face.

I don't like that look. He's much better when we are goofing around and being childish.

Rome stands, offering his hand to Declan. "Thank you for getting Frank's son some help."

I expect Declan to brush off the thanks or give a simple nod of his head, but my brother's lower lip quivers when he meets Rome's gaze. "Did my brother really do all of this?"

Rome presses his lips together, no doubt unsure how to answer.

In lieu of speaking, Rome's arms move slowly until they are wrapped around Declan's form.

Declan's in-charge demeanor cracks in Rome's arms.

His head rests on Rome's shoulder as tears wet his lashes. Declan doesn't have words for his grief, but that doesn't stop the sadness from making itself heard in our childhood home.

Rome holds my brother as he breaks under the weight of all that life has put on his shoulders. Rome's hand moves in a circle over Declan's back. "I'm your brother now. We'll get through this. I'll make sure of it."

It's the perfect thing to say, because now I'm crying, finally feeling bits and pieces of the shock that begin to settle in the air around me.

The two stand like that, hugging while Declan weeps for the state of our ruined family. He doesn't let go until the gurney comes out with the little boy lain on it, still unconscious.

"That's my cue," Declan says, hiccupping through his tears as he swipes at his cheeks. "Thanks, Rome."

Rome kisses my brother's cheek before letting go.

I can't look away, transfixed at the sight of the little boy, so helpless and small.

Was I that small the first time I was taken?

My gaze drinks in the grieving father who can't even feel proper relief yet, because his child is not out of the woods.

Did my father cry when I was found from my three abductions?

"I'll call you with any updates," Declan promises. Then

he leans down and kisses my forehead before he nods at our father and exits out the front door with the other medical professionals.

The bustle of the room dies in an instant, leaving only Orlando, Rome, my father and me in the house with more questions than we have answers.

Or maybe we have questions because we don't like the answers we have.

The sheriff sits in his easy chair while Orlando moves around in the kitchen. My father's large hands scrub over his face. "I can't believe that just happened."

I should offer up a nod or something, but I have no social skills anymore. "Did you cry? When they found me, did you cry like Frank?"

My father's head turns to me, showcasing the bags under his eyes. "Did I cry?"

I nod. "Were you scared?" I tug on my fingers. "I was scared."

The sheriff leans forward, his elbows on his knees. "Was? No, Coco. I am. I never stop being scared. It's probably why I overreacted and sent you far, far away. I was more scared of you dying than I was of you hating me. Still am." He fixes me with a hard stare. "Now you listen to me, and you listen good. I didn't mean to hit you, but I still did. But don't you dare let me off the hook for that. If you don't hate me till my dying day, then I'll know I've truly failed. No one's allowed to hit you—even by mistake."

I don't know why his words strike me as comical, but a small portion of tension between us is released. "Noted. At your funeral, I'll make sure to tell everyone to eat pea soup in your honor."

His face sours. "I hate pea soup."

I offer up what I hope looks like a small smile. "I know."

Though nothing could possibly be funny, my father snorts at my poor attempt at a joke. "Well, good." He points to Rome. "I apologized to your... your boyfriend outside, but you should hear it, too." He squares his shoulders to Rome. "I'm sorry I hit you, Son. Your father would be ashamed of me. When I catch up with him on the other side, I'll let him match me bruise for bruise of what I gave you."

"Forgiven," Rome replies without hesitation.

Orlando comes into the living room, setting a handful of pills in my father's hand and giving him a glass of water. "I'm guessing you didn't take these when you were supposed to. Eventful day."

My father sighs and then knocks back the entire handful. It sounds like he's swallowing a fistful of marbles.

I frown at Orlando. "How do you know what my father takes?"

Orlando shrugs. "Lucky guess." He moves to stand at the front window, drawing the shades.

My father points at Orlando. "He's been at the house every day since you left. He's been looking after me."

I sit up straighter. "Orlando?"

Rome doesn't look surprised. When Orlando's mouth refuses to open, Rome fills me in. "When you and I left, Orlando and I agreed that he would look after your father until you came home—if you decided to ever come home."

My mouth falls open. "Why?"

Orlando leans against the wall, peering out the crack in the curtain with his arms crossed over his chest. "It's your father. You're my mate. That's how this sort of thing works."

As if my heart can take another swell of emotion. Tears well in my eyes as I stand. "You did that for me?"

"Made sure he took his pills. Talked to his doctor to make sure he was eating what he should. Stayed with him when he couldn't get out of bed." He waves off the altruism as if it all amounts to no big deal. "Things like that."

I turn my head to my father. "When couldn't you get out of bed?"

"Most days," Orlando answers at the same time my father says, "He's exaggerating."

My chin angles to my father and then to Orlando, who I know will tell me the truth. "What do you mean?"

Orlando shrugs without looking at me. "It's cancer, Coco. It's only going to get worse. If I stay on him about his pills, then he can move around easier, but it's still bad. I give him a little halluci-mend for the pain, which seems to be the only thing that keeps him from being bedridden."

I can't piece through my grief. There's too much of it to make sense of just yet. But when an idea slides into place, I know I can't ignore it.

I also know that if I stop to think it through, I won't do it.

I hold Rome's hand, giving his fingers a light squeeze. "I have to move in here and take care of my father," I tell him. "I want to run away with you, but I know I'll regret it if I could have been there for my family, and I wasn't."

The sheriff scoffs at me. "Orlando's being dramatic. I'm upright, aren't I? Before this night went up in flames, I was awake enough for a movie, wasn't I?"

The fact that a movie is his version of being active is telling.

My father shakes his head. "No. You should go live your life. I sent you away when you were sick. You shouldn't stay with me when I'm sick. It's not... I don't deserve that. Nature's giving me exactly what I deserve, and I'm taking it without complaining."

Rome looks at me as if I am the best thing in his life. "I'll have your things moved over here tonight." Then Rome stares down my father. "Where she goes, I go. I will not be parted from my mate. Like it or not, I'll be moving in here, too."

My father's upper lip curls. "Don't go saying permanent

things like that about my daughter. I'm telling you, I've been through enough today."

Rome can't resist pushing my father just a little bit further. "Should I start calling you 'Dad'?"

The sheriff grumbles, but doesn't say anything to the contrary, so I know that's exactly what Rome is going to start doing.

The sheriff leans back in his comfy seat, closing his eyes not because any of us are going to get a modicum of peace tonight, but because he cannot take anything more.

I know the feeling.

Orlando moves over to my father's easy chair and helps him to stand. "You can't fall asleep in your chair. You know how it hurts your back." He turns his chin over his shoulder to speak to Rome. "You got her, I've got him."

Rome nods, kissing my temple before he parts from my side. "I'll change the sheets in the guest bedroom. Nico will bring over your things, but for now, you should rest."

There is no rest for the storm in my soul tonight. But knowing that I am not alone in this is enough to convince me that, though I don't have all the answers today, perhaps tomorrow will make more sense to us all.

20

DECLAN'S THEORY

The morning after Fintan was arrested and Frank's son was returned to him, the world still didn't make a whole lot of sense. Or perhaps it did, but I haven't wanted to accept it. Even three weeks after the mayhem, I still can't wrap my mind around it all.

My days have fallen into a rhythm with my father. We don't talk about Fintan or the incident where my father accidentally punched me in the head. Because of that unspoken understanding, we actually get along pretty well.

Of course, that could be because my father has been deteriorating at a rapid pace. No matter what pills he takes or how many, it seems there is no putting off the inevitable. It's only the halluci-mend Orlando gives him that fends off his more brutal aches and pains.

I should be sad about it all, and I probably am, but I

can't seem to find my focus to choose only one thing to be upset about, so I've gone mostly numb. I get my father's medications together in the morning, set his clothes out and take him for a walk. I cook and clean for him and make sure he gets out of bed, if only for a half an hour at a time.

I itch the medical mask I wear most of the time when I am in my father's house now. Once I kick this stomach bug that's been bothering me, I won't have to disinfect the house as often.

Declan and Lucas come in through the front door without knocking. We've taken to coming and going as quietly as possible, so as not to disturb the sheriff if he is resting.

Lucas beelines for me, scooping me in a hug in the middle of the kitchen. My brother's boyfriend is good like that. He doesn't make me talk about anything I don't want to. He simply hugs me and offers help.

He's perfect.

Still, I pull away after a beat. "You shouldn't hug me. I threw up once already this morning."

Lucas rubs his hand up and down my arm, braving the flu I've been warring. "Darn stomach bug?"

"Darn stomach bug."

"I'm glad you're wearing a mask. Better safe than sorry." He glances over his shoulder at Declan as he speaks to me. "How long have you been queasy?"

I want to lean in and take Lucas up on the hug, but that would be selfish, since I'm sick and all. I don't want to pass it to him. "A few days now. I'll go to the doctor at some point. And I'm sure the second I go everything will have cleared up. Every morning, I'm ralphing my brains out, but then by the afternoon, it's like I was never sick." I shake my head at my body. "Whatever."

Lucas shoots Declan a meaningful look. "Interesting."

Declan's grave expression isn't altogether unusual, given the month we've had, but this is more than melancholy. "I heard it." He has a grocery bag in his hand that he clutches as if it carries a deep, dark secret inside.

I tap my medical mask. "Don't worry. I wear this around the sheriff, and whenever I prepare his food. Everything is disinfected a million times a day, so I don't pass anything to him."

Lucas is bright as sunshine when he turns back to me. "You ready for your meetings today?" Lucas asks me, peering into the pan to see what I am cooking.

"Probably. I don't think it matters all that much. The proposals are there. I'm not in the mood to screw around. Either the prime minister signs the bill to add vampire medical education to med schools or he will commit political suicide. You know how I work."

A waft of bacon hits my nose, causing my stomach to lurch. "Would you mind stirring this for a minute, Lucas? The smell is just..."

Lucas chuckles as he takes the spatula from me so he can stir the eggs in the pan and keep an eye on the bacon. "Not a problem." He tilts his head sympathetically. "Did you not sleep well?"

The dark circles under my eyes have been a permanent fixture as of late. "Not particularly. It's fine. I'm sure none of us are sleeping all that great these days. But you're sweet to ask."

Declan plops down on the stool at the counter, the mystery grocery bag in his lap as he cradles his head in his hands. "How's Dad doing?"

Declan and Lucas come to stay with the sheriff whenever I have to leave the house to work or meet with politicians to push for policy change. Luckily, I've been able to do most of that over the phone, but every now and then, I have to go out of the house and meet with someone in person.

I jerk my chin toward the sheriff's bedroom. "Rome is helping him get dressed. The nurse who bathes him couldn't come this morning, so Rome volunteered to help out."

Declan's expression softens, his hand going over his heart. "He's doing all that? Man, we're lucky to have him. That's... He's a good guy."

"Agreed. I didn't even ask him to do that. He saw that I was going to do it, and he told me he could take care of it instead."

Declan leans back. "I'll call the agency and make sure they have a replacement ready for the days the nurse can't come out. You shouldn't have to deal with that. You're doing enough."

I shrug. "I've lost the ability to feel stress. I know it's there, but there's so much of it that it cancels itself out somehow."

Declan watches me more carefully than I am used to. "That's probably not healthy. Maybe I can take a week of vacation days and stay here so you and Rome can get away. You need a break, Coco-bean."

I move around the counter and sit beside him on the other stool. "I think we all need a break, but now is not the time. Save your vacation days for an actual vacation. Plan something fun with Lucas and go nuts. I don't think I could take it if you got old, too."

Declan lowers his chin. "I knew Dad would go downhill quick without chemo, but I didn't expect it to be this fast. I thought we might have another week or two before he couldn't bathe or dress himself. It was wishful thinking."

I thought so, too, but hope doesn't always pan out.

The sheriff's energy has depleted, and there's no end in sight. It's like as soon as Fintan was outed as the root of all our problems, his spirit diminished, leaving him bereft, weak and sad.

But we don't talk about it, so it doesn't exist.

My father's weakness must be airborne, because I've been sleeping in, not hungry and I've had this stomach bug I can't shake.

But even though the smell of eggs makes me nauseous now, I knew that was the breakfast I should make. My father hasn't been hungry lately, but I know I can tempt him to eat with bacon and eggs. Now that there's no point in eating healthy, I figure any calories are good calories.

Rome comes out of my father's bedroom with a grim look on his face. He doesn't say anything because we both know my father is on the cusp of needing more help than we are qualified to give. He kisses my temple and nods to Declan and Lucas. "Morning."

Declan responds by getting off his stool and hugging Rome in that rough, brotherly way that shakes the dust off my soul. "Thank you," Declan chokes out. "You can call me next time, and I'll come over and take care of him."

Rome rubs a slow circle across Declan's back. "It's no trouble. I never got to do that stuff for my own father. Elias is the closest thing to a dad I've got. I don't mind taking care of him."

As if I could love him any more than I already do.

Rome releases Declan from the hug and reaches for the grocery bag on the counter. "Are these the vitamins for your dad?"

He dumps out the contents of the bag while Declan cringes. "Uh, yes but..."

There on the counter is the bottle of super strength vitamins for my father, sitting on the counter beside...

My nose scrunches. "Is that a pregnancy test?" I glance up at Declan, utterly perplexed. "You bought a pregnancy test? Why would you need one of those?"

Declan presses his lips together, taking a beat before responding. "Well, I was going to have this conversation with you in private, but I guess Rome should be here for this. And Lucas helped me pick it out, so he's already aware of my suspicions."

I tilt my head at him. It's as if he's dumped a unicycle on the counter and expected me to make sense of why anyone in this family might have a use for such a thing. "I don't get it."

Declan pinches the bridge of his nose. "How long have you had this stomach bug, Coco?"

I shrug. "A few days."

"Are you and Rome having sex?"

I shoot him a wry look. "You know we are." I balk at the test. "That's for me? You think I..."

I haven't laughed in weeks, but that tips it. A loud cackle erupts out of me, filling the room until my eyes water. "Declan, you're ridiculous. Precious, but ridiculous. Rome and I can't get pregnant. You know that. Vampires and humans can't procreate. That's not a thing."

Declan waits until my laughter crests. It's then I realize Rome has gone completely still.

Lucas turns off the stove and migrates to my side. "Hear him out, Colette."

Declan keeps his voice low as he stands before me, laying out his theory. "Vampires and humans have never procreated. There's a difference between *haven't* and *can't*. We don't know what vampires and humans can do together because you're the first two who have tried. We didn't know humans could mate and share the vampire bond, but that's all kinds of possible, as you've proven." Declan motions to the test, shaking his head. "Look, maybe I'm wrong. But this is the quickest way to find out."

"You're wrong," I rule, not bothering to beat around the bush. "It's not possible."

Declan raises his hands in surrender. "Then take the test and prove me wrong. You want me to start asking questions about your cycle? Because we can go that route."

I grimace at the notion of discussing something that personal with my brother and his boyfriend. "What day is it? I have no concept of a calendar anymore."

Lucas rattles off the date.

I try to think back to the last cycle I had, but the past month or so has been a blur. I went from disappearing to the cabin where time had no meaning, to caring for the sheriff full-time, where the days pass with little change or noteworthiness.

My mouth pulls to the side. "Fine. Give me the dang

test. You're wrong, but if science needs to tell you that, fine by me."

Rome hasn't moved. I'm not sure he has blinked.

I touch his hand after I snatch up the test from the counter. "Rome, it's not true. It's not possible. Don't freak out. There's nothing to worry about."

Rome turns his head to me but doesn't speak. I'm not sure he can.

Before his fear can leap onto me, I move into the bathroom, very aware that three men are waiting for me to pee on a stick.

It's not true. I know it's not. I made my peace long ago with the fact that I would never carry a child because the plan was always for my mother's lethal bloodline to die with me.

I'm not nervous. At least, that's what I tell myself when I take off my medical mask and stare at the stick, waiting for it to tell me what I know to be true.

It's not possible. That's a solid fact I never had to question. Rome is the perfect man for me in so many ways— one of which being that he can never get me pregnant.

But when two pink lines appear on the end of the stick, the world I thought I understood cracks open, sending me into an abyss of uncertainty.

21

WALKING WITH THE SHERIFF

I haven't spoken in half an hour. I don't want to talk about what is certainly a faulty pregnancy test. False positives happen all the time, I bet.

The second I emerged from the bathroom, I got my father's shoes on him and decided now would be a good time for his walk.

The air is crisp and the world is quiet under its blanket of snow, which is a good thing because I don't want to hear a single word.

"You're quiet this morning," the sheriff remarks as we make our way down his street.

"Too much on my mind and nothing worth talking about," I tell him. "Declan and I are having a little misunderstanding."

The sheriff nods. "I'm sure you two will work it out."

"We're not fighting," I clarify. "He thinks the sky is

green, while I know the sky is blue. See? Misunderstanding. Declan is wrong. He'll see."

Because if Declan is right, then that opens a whole new can of worms.

So he's wrong, plain and simple.

We walk mostly in silence around the block, taking our time because my father isn't all that steady on his feet these days. The walk is the most exercise his body can tolerate, but I know that the first day he talks me out of going, it will be the last day he gets fresh air.

And today I really need some fresh air.

"Slower," the sheriff begs, tugging on my arm.

I didn't realize my need to get away from that pregnancy test was quickening my steps, but when I slow, I worry I am too close to the very wrong verdict.

It's a false positive. There's nothing more to it.

"Have you heard anything about Fintan's hearing?" my father asks, shivering even though he is tucked in a winter coat with a hat, scarf and gloves.

I guess we can talk about that. Though we've been avoiding the subject of our rogue family member, I will gladly discuss Fintan's villainy instead of that defunct pregnancy test.

"They're rushing everything through because it's us. The hearing is next week."

My father nods. "I don't want to go."

"I wasn't going to suggest it. I think since Fintan went

rogue on this one, he can stand there and be sentenced on his own, too."

The sheriff shakes his head, his cheeks finally getting a little color from the snowy chill. "I still can't believe I didn't see it. None of it. Ten years ago, I didn't realize it was him who took you. But he knew your schedule, your location. It all adds up. I can't decide which part of me I'm more ashamed of—the father or the cop."

His frustration is not far from my own. "None of us knew. He did a good job of hiding it from us."

"But it's more than that. He knew how hard we've been working to get all traces of halluci-blend out of the West End, yet he was making it himself this whole time." He shakes his head again. "To kidnap a little boy? To kidnap his own sister?"

I swallow hard. I want to beg my father to stop talking about this, but he should talk about it all. It's good to vent about the unthinkable.

I'm the one who's being a big baby about it.

I clear my throat. "You couldn't have known."

"Where was he cooking the stuff? They didn't find the ingredients for cooking halluci-blend in Fairfax's house when they went in to investigate. I need to call the guys who brought Fintan in to see if they got that information out of him. I want the entire operation shut down." He glares at the snowdrifts on the curb. "I'm telling you, Coco, if I die before this entire thing is put to rest, there will be no peace for me in the afterlife."

"The afterlife?" I've never heard my father talk about that before.

"Sure. Heaven. Hell. All that stuff. I have to know there won't be a trace of halluci-blend left to bleed into the West End. I can't leave this world worse than I found it."

For so long, he was the kind of cop who did exactly that. He looked the other way when the West End needed help, and only served to populate the prison with vampires, instead of building up the community or getting to the root of the issues. To see remorse on him now is refreshing, but entirely too late to do the world much good.

"I think the system is going to make sure Fintan pays for his crimes."

"That's mighty big of you to say, being that one of his crimes was against you. You don't want revenge?"

It's an odd question from my father, so I take my time mulling it over before responding. "I mean, I shot him in the leg and then in the knee. If that's not a decent attempt at evening the score for all he put me through, then I don't want to know what is."

My father snorts at my logic. "I suppose that's fair." His chin hardens as we continue our walk. "I sent the wrong kid away. I sent you to Lonmure, when I should have sent Fintan to prison."

I shoot him a wry look. "I think we can agree you didn't have all the facts."

Then my father does something so unexpected, I have to look down to verify with my eyes that it is actually happening.

The Sheriff of Mayfield reaches out and holds my hand.

Warmth spreads through me, heightening our connection to include actual affection, which is a new twist for us both. We don't talk about it. We don't acknowledge it is happening. For this single, solitary moment, we walk in forgiveness, letting that light guide the way home.

22

THE SHERIFF'S LAST STAND

The moment we step over the threshold, I can tell the atmosphere has not lightened in the slightest since I took my father on his morning walk. I guess asking the three men pacing in the living room to have forgotten about the false positive on my pregnancy test is too much to ask.

My plan is to ignore their worry completely and go about my day, but that doesn't seem to be a possibility when my father calls the guys out on their palpable concern. "What's wrong?

"What's wrong?" Declan asks, incredulous. "Where do we start?"

Rome fixes his eyes on me. His voice carries a deadly calm to it that stiffens my spine. "You didn't have your phone on you. How am I supposed to get ahold of you if you don't have your phone?"

I lock eyes with him, silently asking just who he thinks he's talking to in that tone of voice.

Rome's nostrils flare but then he backs down, lowering his chin. "Apologies. I couldn't reach you, and I was panicking."

I help my father sit in his easy chair in the living room, keeping my eyes on the task while I talk to Rome who is standing between the living room and the kitchen. "You knew where I was. I was on a walk with my father. Is there a problem?" Before he opens his mouth to respond, I clarify. "Is there a real problem, and not an imagined one?"

At this, my father turns his head to the three men in the kitchen. "What's going on? What did I miss?"

"Nothing," I promise.

Declan stomps into the living room. "Will you listen to your boyfriend? We've got a problem. Several, in fact. The precinct called your phone while you were out, Dad."

My father settles into his chair. "I'm sure they did. I didn't tell them why I retired, only that I was out. A few of the officers weren't too happy about my sudden departure."

"That's not it." Declan paces around the living room, and for the first time I see the worry setting in deep. "Dad, you need to stay put. No more walks, no nothing. Not until we get this situation under control."

My father's nose crinkles. "What situation?"

Declan levels his gaze at the sheriff. "They don't know how, but Fintan has escaped."

Everything stills in my mind because Declan's words cannot possibly be true. My brother explains the phone call that came through while we were on our walk, but still, I cannot wrap my mind all the way around the crisis.

Declan locks all the doors and draws the curtains shut while Lucas stays by my side like a sentry.

Now I'm the one who's pacing. Back and forth, I walk across the living room, anxiety spiking every few seconds. "How did this happen?"

Rome is making phone calls. He hasn't stopped for a solid five minutes. He's in heavy planning mode, and isn't likely to stop anytime soon.

Lucas only leaves my side to pack a bag of clothes for my father. He comes out of the sheriff's bedroom with determination on his face. "I think we should get going and make a plan on the way. This is the last place we should be if Fintan is on the loose."

My father hasn't risen from his easy chair. After one call to the precinct, he has been silent, staring ahead without making any effort to leave his home.

I stop pacing to stare at Lucas. "Get going where? I'm thinking the best place to be is right here. Or at my house. If Fintan's escaped and he wants to find me, might as well do this now."

Lucas presses his lips together as if praying for patience. "Declan, I'm loading up the car. We can go to my house, since Fintan won't think to look for her there."

Declan nods once. "That's a good idea. Thanks, Lucas." He pinches the bridge of his nose. "I'm sorry this is happening. I don't want to bring you into our family drama."

Lucas doesn't waffle. "Your family is my family. That's how we work."

"I'm not leaving," I tell the room at large as I cross to where I've hung my purse. I fish out my gun and make sure the thing is loaded. "When Fintan comes for me, I'll send him right back to jail."

At this, my father speaks up. "Where he'll escape all over again." He looks up at me, his jaw firm with frustration. "How did he escape?"

"You said the precinct reported he escaped enroute to the courthouse where he was going to be sentenced."

"Yes, but how? In all my years on the force, not once did a prisoner escape." My father shakes his head. "I've got a bad feeling about this, kids."

Declan stands at my side. "You think he had help on the inside? You think someone on the force helped Fintan escape?"

The sheriff touches his chin while he thinks. "It's the only explanation. I don't know which one let him loose. It's not like Fintan was in top physical shape. He had two gunshot wounds in his leg."

My face pales as my father's logic sounds more and more like sworn fact. "Any ideas who it might be?"

The sheriff shrugs, but I can tell he's got a hypothesis.

His silence speaks volumes, giving me time to think. My father knows which cops gave him pushback when it came to policing fairly. He knows who isn't completely onboard with the concept of vampires holding equal rights.

He knows whom he's chatted with about my location, my safety. He knows whose numbers Fintan has programmed on his phone.

"Lampert," my father whispers.

Declan's face pulls. "He's an annoying suck up, but he's your second in command, Dad. You really think he's the leak?"

"Jaren Lampert is friends with Fintan, enough to share information. Enough to spring him free. Lampert is in charge, now that I've retired." He glances to Rome. "Lampert has opinions on vampire rights. He wasn't a fan of the policy change when I told my people they couldn't arrest vampires for possession anymore. Now they have to give them the option of rehab for a first offense, just like the humans get."

Declan's chin lowers. "I thought Lampert was sucking

up to you when he started hanging out with Fintan in his spare time."

My father reaches for his phone on the coffee table with renewed energy. "Frank is at risk. Lampert knows it's him who turned on Fintan. Frank is the one who can point the finger at Fintan for pushing the drugs on him and kidnapping his son. And not just Fintan. If Fintan was working with others, Frank or his son could identify them all."

Declan reaches for his keys. "I'll go pick up Frank and his son. I'm guessing Fintan will either go for Coco to take her blood, or he'll go for the two people who can put him in prison for life."

The sheriff nods. "Where will you take them?"

Declan shakes his head. "Best you don't know. Best no one knows." He turns to Rome, who is still standing in the center of the kitchen. "You got Coco?"

Rome nods. "We're going away. Far away."

Declan gives Rome a thumbs up. "Good." He kisses my forehead in lieu of saying goodbye.

The sheriff lifts his voice to get Declan's attention. "Declan?"

My brother turns, pausing his exit only for our father. "Yeah, Dad?"

"I love you, Son. With all my stupid heart. I couldn't be more proud of you. Be good to Lucas."

"Always am, Dad."

"Be good to yourself, too."

Declan's shoulders lower. "Thanks, Dad. Will do."

While Declan and Lucas converse quietly near the front door, Rome glances at the sheriff. "I'm sorry, Elias, but I can't risk her being anywhere Fintan could find her. Lucas packed up your things; you're coming with us."

The sheriff's jaw firms. "I'm not running from my own kid."

"Well, we are. If Coletta and I are gone, no one is here to take care of you, so you're coming with us."

The sheriff presses his hand to the coffee table. "No. This is my mess because Fintan is my son, and he's out of hand. If he comes here looking for Coco, I will handle it."

I want to question everything my father just said, but Rome doesn't have time for conversations. "I understand. I'll have Nico stay here with you, then."

I balk at the suggestion. "Nico?"

Rome already has his phone pressed to his ear. "Nico can handle firing on Fintan if he steps into the house. He'll be glad for the opportunity."

My palms are sweating as my heart pounds. "No. I'll stay with my father. I'm not going to leave him with Nico."

Rome's stubborn nature flares in time with my own. "Well, I'm not leaving my pregnant girlfriend at the one place where she's bound to be targeted. Orlando's tied up with things in the West End, so he can't get here right now. Nico will do in a pinch."

I cringe at those words hitting the air. "I'm not..."

But the damage has already been done.

My father gapes at me, his eyes round. "You're what?"

I roll my eyes but Declan chimes in as he tugs on his jacket. "She took a pregnancy test this morning. It's positive. We didn't think it was possible for a vampire and a human to procreate, but apparently that's only because no one has ever tried before. Coco is pregnant, so she's not staying where Fintan can find her." He zips up his jacket. "I don't care about anything but keeping my niece or nephew protected." He points at my stomach. "That's potentially the new Last Deadblood in there, if it's a girl. We pull no punches. Rome, you tell Nico he has my blessing to aim to kill."

Rome nods, but we both know Nico needs no one's blessing to blow away the person responsible for pushing halluci-blend into the West End.

The sheriff rises with ample discomfort voiced. "That's... You're carrying my grandbaby?"

I chew on my lower lip. "We're not talking about this. It's not real. Fintan coming here might be real, though, so we need to leave."

The sheriff's upper lip curls, his head turning to Rome. "You're right, Son. Take her out of here. Keep your phone on you. Declan and I will keep you posted. Send Nico. Tell Orlando the plan. Communication stops there."

Rome nods in thanks as he presses his phone to his ear.

"I'm not accustomed to running, but the game has changed." Then he directs his conversation to Nico in short half-sentences.

I stand in the center of the living room, trying not to let nerves take me down when a clear head is needed.

I'm not pregnant. I can't be.

But that's not the thing to focus on right now. I have to get out of here.

"Leaving you feels counterintuitive," I tell my father, who doesn't seem the least bit foggy right now.

"Hopefully you'll only be gone for the evening. Nico and I will take care of Fintan. We'll send him right back to jail. After you go, I will reach out to an officer who will hold Lampert back for questioning. Fintan didn't escape on his own. Especially not with an injured leg." He reaches into the pouch on the side of his easy chair and pulls out his gun.

"You can't be serious."

The sheriff motions me toward the exit. "You can't be serious, thinking I won't defend my grandchild when the baby has come under attack. You'll be gone a day or so, then when you get back, I'm marching you straight to the doctor, so he can do his thing and make sure the baby is okay."

"Sheriff, I…"

He holds his hand up to stop my protest. "You want to see me surly, keep on backtalking. That baby needs to be seen by a doctor. You need to be on prenatal vitamins. While you're out, make sure you pick some up."

This whole thing has spun out of control. "I can't leave you! Does no one see that? You need someone here who can help you." My heart pounds because this is all moving in the wrong direction.

The sheriff meets my eyes with a firmness I surely inherited from him. "You have to let me go, kid."

Of all the things he could say to me, that is the one that hurts the most. I can't let him go. We have too many unfinished heartaches between us to call it a day and walk away. I've never wanted to fight with him as much as I do now, if only to hear him care about me, to know my father's heart bleeds for me.

I need to lock in my brain the fact that my father cares about me.

My lower lip trembles at the truth that's hard to hear. My father needs me. He can't fix himself food or get his meds without help. I don't want to let him go. I don't want to leave him to fight this final battle on his own.

Rome is bustling around, packing and preparing us to leave for however many days it takes to get Fintan and his accomplice behind bars.

My father raises his voice. "Rome, come here."

I can tell Rome doesn't want to comply, but he trots to the patriarch without complaint. "What can I get you, Elias?"

My father points to the couch. "Sit down. I have to talk to you." He waits until Rome sits, and then he lays down the law. "You need to know a few things before you go."

"I'm listening."

My father's gaze bores straight through Rome's tough exterior, piercing my boyfriend's tender soul. "Don't let this city destroy all the good things about you, Son. Take my daughter and my grandbaby out of Mayfield as often as you can. Let them see that there's a whole big, wide world out there for them to explore. Let them see that minds can be open. Let them see there's more to life than this. Than being chased. Hunted."

Tenderness glistens in Rome's eyes while I stand in stunned silence, listening to my father pass down the wisdom he has acquired from his years of trying to figure out life. "Yes, Sir. I can do that."

"Listen to your wife, Son." The sheriff waves off any protest that might arise, being that we legally can't get married. "I know she's as good as being your wife, and so do you. Listen to her. No one else does. They think they know what's best for her, but where I went wrong is that I didn't listen to her. I panicked when I became a husband. I thought I knew what was best, but I forgot to listen to my wife. I forgot I'm not in this alone." He leans forward. "You are not in this alone, Rome."

Though I have tears in my eyes, I don't expect anything could possibly make Rome emotional. But when he replies, his voice is gravelly. "I panic, too. My people will die if I don't protect her. *I* will die if I don't protect her."

My father's voice quiets. "Do it because you love her, not because you're afraid. There's a difference. I forgot that. Don't make the same mistake. Love makes you listen. Fear makes you run. We don't need any more cowards in this family."

Rome pauses, letting the wisdom sink in before he nods. "Thank you."

The sheriff sits back and flips his hand toward the door. "Now get on out. I'll take it from here. Tell Nico to stay home. I want that boy far away from this. Orlando, too."

I don't understand why he won't accept the protection. "You should really let them come and be with you."

The sheriff shakes his head. "I've got this, Coco. I love you, honey. If I haven't said it so you've heard it, hear it now. I love you."

Confusion hits my system. We don't talk like that. I wouldn't even know how to say those words to my father, or if they would be true if I did.

Instead of echoing the sentiment, I meet him as far as I can. "I hear you, Dad."

I never call him "Dad". He's always the sheriff or my father.

A twinkle glistens in his eyes as he nods at me. "Go on, now."

Rome loads up the car while I stand in the center of the living room, mute and very afraid. It's not myself I fear for right now. My father... The way he's talking...

When Rome ushers me out the front door, my chest tightens with the worry that I just saw my father for the last time.

23

FATHER AND FINTAN

Rome keeps his car going at the exact speed limit as he drives us out of Mayfield. I don't know where we are headed, but he is making sure we don't get pulled over before we get there.

"Your father is right. You need to see a doctor the second we get back."

"I'm not..." But instead of finishing that sentence by denying that I'm pregnant, I close my eyes and lean my head against the seat. "I can't keep the baby, Rome. We both know it."

The car jerks, but Rome gets himself under control. "Explain."

"*I* am the Last Deadblood. Even if I'd fallen for a human where getting pregnant was more of a possibility, I wasn't ever going to risk it. I can't have a girl, Rome. If I do, she's at risk, and so is the entire vampire population." I turn my chin away from him. "I made that choice a long time ago. I didn't think it was possible with you."

To his credit, Rome fights to keep his voice calm, leaving a beat of silence between my verdict and his reply. "I can protect you and our baby."

I chew on my lower lip. "I know. That's what makes this so hard. I never let myself believe this was possible for me. Now that it is?" I shake my head as the last of my hard-won denial slips away. "I don't know what to do. I know what I should do to protect your people. But I don't know if I can." I close my eyes. "I don't know."

Rome reaches out and holds my hand, connecting us when I feel lost in my abyss of uncertainty. "Then for today, we don't make any decisions. We listen to your father and protect each other out of love, not out of fear. We make decisions as if Mayfield doesn't exist."

"But it very much does."

Rome motions out the window. "Not out here. We're outside the city limits."

I guess we are.

Rome squeezes my hand. "I vote that we don't worry about Mayfield when we're not in Mayfield."

My shoulders lower. "I think I can get onboard with that, at least for today."

Rome exhales. "Good. Let's deal with one giant thing at a time."

As if on cue, his phone rings. He sighs before answering. "Yeah?"

But the conversation isn't directed at Rome. I hear my father's voice echoing through the Bluetooth in the car, but it isn't spoken near enough to the phone. "Fintan, you know you shouldn't be here."

My spine stiffens as fear trills through my body.

Rome mutes our end of the call, so we can listen without becoming a distraction. Then he turns on a recording app that will chronicle this phone call in case it proves useful to the authorities. His knuckles whiten as he grips the steering wheel tighter.

"Where is she?" my brother asks. Fintan sounds like he might be a few feet away from the sheriff. I can picture him standing in the doorway, limping toward my father in the living room.

My voice turns shrill as it becomes clear that there will be little effort put forth of Fintan pretending he has a conscience.

Panic zips through my veins. "Turn the car around, Rome!"

But Rome keeps on the course, passing the next exit without moving toward it. "We can't. I have to keep you and our baby safe. Driving you straight toward the man who wants to abduct you and sell your blood isn't going to happen."

"But my father is alone with him! This isn't going to end well. I have to stop it!"

Rome truly does look torn, but he keeps the car driving away from my father. "No. I love you, Coletta. This is what that looks like. It means that when there's a criminal trying to find you, I don't drive you straight into his clutches."

Darn his solid logic. It goes against both of our needs to stand and fight.

I guess we don't have that option anymore, not when there might be a baby on the way.

It's the first time it dawns on me that I might actually be pregnant. My hand goes to my stomach as my body floods with a fierce protectiveness that pushes out a portion of my fear.

My gaze climbs to Rome. "If Fintan finds out about the baby, he will try to take the child from us. If it's a girl, he will never stop coming after her."

Rome reaches over and holds my hand. "One thing at a time. First things first: call in Fintan's location to the police. I can't use my phone. It has to be you."

"You want me to call the cops who let Fintan escape?"

Rome shrugs. "It's our only hope at setting things right. All we can do is follow the law. It's up to them to do their part."

I text Declan the information so I don't miss any of the exchange between my father and Fintan, telling my brother to call the cops so they can arrest Fintan.

My father's voice crackles through the car. "Your sister is none of your concern anymore. How could you, Fintan? How could you kidnap her like that? How could you hurt her the way you did?"

Fintan's growl holds a modicum of pain to it. "I gave them strict instructions not to hurt her, back when she was fifteen and we saw our window. They weren't supposed to hurt her, only take her blood so we could sell it and make our mint. But she kept trying to escape, and they got carried away."

"That's how you justify this?"

Fintan scoffs. "My trust from Mom was still locked up back then! I couldn't get my hands on the money that was mine. I had to do something."

"Money?" I can picture my father's upper lip curling. "That's all this has been about? You sold out your sister for something as common as money?"

Fintan's patience appears to be wearing thin. "Where is she? You know I might not have much time before the cops catch up with me."

"You brought Jaren Lampert in on this. He was my partner. Why?"

Fintan's reply is snide. "Two words: government salary."

My father's scoff echoes my own. "You ran through your inheritance from your mother in the first two years you got your hands on it. There will never be enough money for you, Fintan. Don't you see that? No matter how much of your sister's blood you sold, it still didn't give you enough money to satisfy."

"I have a plan, old man. A plan that could set us up for life."

"Sell more of your sister's blood? Take her away from her family and treat her like an animal?"

Angst wells up in my throat. There aren't tears enough for this.

Fintan laughs. "You think I didn't learn from thinking small ten years ago when I had her where I wanted her? I've got a buyer now who could set me up for life. Set us all up."

The sheriff scoffs. "Do you think Declan or I would take money made that way? And what buyer? Is this all part of some crazy plan that will never pan out?"

Why is my father asking for tips on how to best sell my blood?

As if Rome can read my mind, he explains quietly, "Elias is baiting Fintan. He's getting all the information from him, so we know who's coming for us."

I can't feel relief. I'm not sure I can feel anything other than terror. To hear my brother speak so casually about abducting me, skipping over the blame regarding my many maladies because he didn't knock me around himself makes my stomach churn.

Fintan's pride takes the sheriff's well-placed bait. "If

you think the revolutionaries will pay top dollar for her blood, you can't imagine what Senator Collins will pay."

My breath catches as the world I thought I knew cracks open and reveals a gaping wound I didn't realize was there this entire time.

The sheriff blows a raspberry at Fintan's declaration. "You're making things up. There's no way he could make a deal with you. He's in jail for trying to take Coco's blood at the governor's mansion—which he failed at, by the way."

Fintan's cadence is rushed. "You'd be surprised how expensive it is to promote the idea of peace. It's cheaper and simpler to let nature play out. If the vampires were exterminated, the senator would have one less headache."

"And he's actually going to pay you for your sister's blood? Even though he's locked up, he can somehow get money to you?" I can picture my father shaking his head. "You're delusional."

Fintan's voice turns grim. "He already did. Lampert made the transaction happen on the Senator's behalf. I was supposed to deliver on my end of the deal, but Colette shot me before I could take her blood." His voice turns choked as emotion shines through. "I have to make good on this delivery, or I'm as good as dead."

"You don't think prison can protect you from the Senator's reach? Fintan, return the money and turn him in!"

Fintan's voice sounds strained with stress. "You truly

think the senator's reach is limited by iron bars? I have to deliver. Tell me where Colette is."

The sheriff sighs. "I think you know I'm not going to give her over to you. Isn't that why you came here? Isn't that why you never cut me in on this sweet deal? Because you knew I would talk you out of it. You're here now, hoping I will talk you out of going through with this." He pauses, and pride for my father's prowess expands in my chest. "Well, here I am, Son. Don't be this man. Don't throw away your family for a buck."

"I'm here for Colette's blood! I don't have much time, Dad!"

"I have hope that you can be more than this. I know you love us. I didn't raise you to care more about money than your family."

Fintan scoffs while I hold myself back from committing to any sort of reaction.

Our father wasn't after money, but he didn't exactly raise us to care about the family.

But that's neither here nor there when I hear the unmistakable sound of the click of a gun readying itself to fire.

"Who's aiming their weapon?" I ask Rome in a tight whisper. "Fintan or the sheriff?"

Rome holds tight to my hand in lieu of a response. When we don't have the answers, all we can do is hold tight to each other while a little family in Mayfield tries to tear itself apart.

Fintan's voice is shrill. "Tell me where Colette is! My life depends on it."

"*Your* life? You created this mess. And your life is not worth more than your sister's. I love all my children equally." Then the sheriff's voice takes on a lilt of annoyance. "Put your gun away Fintan. I taught you how to shoot that thing; I'm not going to die by it."

Even though I cannot see the two in the living room of my father's house, I know Fintan isn't taking the sheriff's scolding seriously. When Fintan wants something, he makes it happen.

"We have to turn around," I tell Rome. Then I shake my head and pull my phone back out of my purse. "I'm calling Fintan."

At this, Rome pulls over onto the side of the freeway. "You can't do that. We are not giving you over to a psychopath. You texted Declan, who is calling in people to arrest Fintan. It's done."

"It's not done! If I don't call Fintan and make a plan for him to see me, he's going to kill my father!"

"If you turn yourself over to Fintan, he's going to kill *you*! And not just you, but an entire race of people, once he gets his hands on an endless supply of your blood." Rome doesn't take my phone from my hand, but trusts that his words will sink in.

Frustration wells up in me as hot tears squeeze out of the corners of my eyes. "I don't know how to fix this!"

"Because it's not for you to fix. Help is on the way to stop Fintan. We have to trust them, Coletta. We have to stay calm and stick to the plan."

My father's voice crackles through the interior of the car. "I won't let you take my daughter, Fintan. Put the gun down, or I start shooting."

My heart pounds as I hold tight to the flimsy belief that somehow this will all work out in the end.

I squinch my eyes shut and pray that Fintan comes to his senses.

Fintan's voice is weighted with despair. "If you can't help me, then I can't risk you turning me in to the cops. I'm sorry, Dad. For what it's worth, I love you. Everything I've done was to make our family's legacy more than an omen of death."

"Then put the gun down, Son. Look. See? I'm unarmed now."

When a gunshot pierces the air, I am positive my own heart has stopped beating.

Rome's gasp is beyond me now. I am positively gone, floating in an abyss of loss and horror.

This is my family.

This is the life I will never escape.

24

LOST TO THE WORLD

Rome uses a fake ID to check us into a hotel far from Mayfield. I'm not sure how many false identities he has, and I don't care. Nothing matters anymore. I can't feel anything, can't hear anything, can't care about anything. Even as Rome carries me into the hotel through the back entrance, I don't care that he is taking me further from my father's body, which is no doubt still bleeding out all over his easy chair.

Rome fumbles with the keycard and then carries me to the bed, lying me atop the mattress with utmost care.

I roll onto my side and curl in a ball, shutting out as much of the world as I possibly can.

Rome is on his phone, talking in short, clipped bursts while keeping his voice quiet, as if he is afraid to wake me.

My entire life is unrecognizable. I had a father not half an hour ago, and now I don't. I never thought I would have to listen to my father breathe his last, but after that phone call, I feel as if part of my soul is lost, lain forfeit at the feet of what was left of my innocence.

Rome does his best to keep the phone calls away from me, stepping into the bathroom to keep me out of the loop as much as possible. Though, I can tell he gets anxious when I am out of his eyeline, because he won't close the bathroom door, and keeps poking his head out to check that I haven't moved.

I have no plans to get out of bed ever again. If I can lift my head on my own, it will be a feat of wonder for which I am not yet equipped.

Time has no meaning. Even as the sun sets, I am unaware if I should care. I don't know if I have missed any significant parts of the day. Nothing is significant right now. The horrors wash over me like white noise, each one cancelling the others out because they are too deafening to comprehend on their own.

Rome is silent when he is not on the phone, communicating with Declan, the police, Orlando and Nico. He even calls the salon to make sure they don't need me for anything, and if they do, to call Orlando.

Though the door is locked, Rome keeps checking it, so I know he is worried we will be found by someone seeking to get their hands on my blood. If I had any sort of sense in my brain right now, I would be worried about that, too. But as it is, I can barely think further than the alarm that keeps sounding off in my head, warning me that my breaking point was several catastrophes ago.

Time passes. I'm not sure how much. Food comes but I don't want any of it. A cup of water is pressed to my lips when Rome sits me up however long later, so I drink.

I taste a little of his blood in the water, and a little of Orlando's from the flask he always keeps filled for me. Normally there would be a kick of endorphins that flood my system upon ingesting their blood, but even that cannot lift my spirits off the bottom of my splattered psyche.

Rome doesn't make me talk because he is smart enough to know there aren't words. When he runs out of people to call and finally tires of pacing, he inclines on the bed beside me. I don't resist when he scoops me to his side, resting my head on the space between his chest and his shoulder. His lips press to my forehead, his warmth a small prayer for me to one day return to myself and to him.

He covers us with the comforter and makes a wall of pillows around us, hemming us in with the fluffy fortress of his making.

I'm not sure if I sleep. Maybe I do. But my dreams are mute, as is my waking. All I know is that I am in Rome's arms, where he will not tolerate anything terrible coming for me. As long as I am in his arms, I don't have to make decisions about what might be growing inside my stomach.

I don't have to think about the corrupt police system that allowed my brother's escape.

I don't have to think about what it means that Fintan is so lost that he murdered our father, or that Fintan wants to sell my blood to make weapons that could exterminate an entire race of people.

I don't have to think about anything.

When my phone rings, Rome answers it.

When my tears come, Rome wipes them away.

When I don't have the words, Rome is quiet and doesn't force them.

I have no idea how long we lay together in the pillow fortress. Maybe hours. Maybe days. But when a knock sounds on the door, I know it is far too soon for anyone to be here, informing us that the rest of the world is still spinning.

When Declan enters, my heart thumps louder. Or perhaps my heart thumps for the first time since my father was shot.

My brother looks like he hasn't slept in weeks. His cheeks are wet, even as Lucas grabs him a tissue from the bathroom upon their entry.

Lucas and Rome speak in hushed voices near the door while Declan collapses onto the second queen-sized bed in our hotel room. His body curls around a pillow while he cries into the sheets.

Declan has always been the more functional of us

three kids. Fintan bulldozes people when he can't get his way. I run away or double down—usually in the wrong order. But Declan feels things. He welcomes the heartbreak even when there might not be a cure for it. His tears soak the bed because he is the most mature of the three of us. He isn't afraid of his own grief.

My grief, on the other hand, feels like a black hole. If I get too near, I might be swallowed whole and never come out of it alive. So I remain numb in my sadness, weighted by the horror of what the world has come to.

I am the rallying point of the world's bigotry. I am the one they will never stop fighting about. As long as my heart beats, not only will I be in danger, but the entire vampire race will be in jeopardy.

I may not have all the answers, but my brain finally focuses in on one solution I haven't let myself consider up until now. I don't want to think about it, but there it is: the only option.

But I know I'll need help, because it's not something I am capable of doing on my own.

"My phone," I rasp. I haven't spoken in a long time, so my throat is not prepared for what my mind is certain I must do. I fight with the comforter and sit up, drawing Rome to my side and away from Lucas.

"What is it, tré-sur? What can I get for you?"

"Your phone," I correct myself. "I need to make a call."

"Of course. You want my phone? Yours is right here. I just turned off the sound so it wouldn't disturb you."

"*Your* phone," I confirm. "I don't think I have Nico's number."

Rome's nose crinkles. "Why do you need to call my brother?"

I shake my head. "I just need to. And I need one minute alone to talk to him."

Rome's mouth firms. "Why? What do you want to say to Nico that I can't hear?"

I take the phone from Rome and connect the call to Nico. I stand on wobbly legs, moving toward the bathroom.

Nico's voice is rushed when he speaks, thinking Rome is calling him. "I'm on it. I'm with Orlando. We're hunting down Fintan as best we can. He was gone when we got to the Kennedy house. We'll find him, Rome."

I turn away from Rome's inquisitive stare, shutting and locking the bathroom door in his face, my voice tremulous. "Nino-bear?" I turn on the fan to drown out my words so Rome can't eavesdrop.

Nico swears. "Colette? I thought you were Rome. Where's my brother? Why do you have his phone?"

I clear my throat, but it doesn't make my voice any steadier. "Nico, I need a favor." I glance up at the exhaust fan, hoping only Nico can hear me over the din.

"Is Rome alright? Why do you have his phone?"

"Rome is with me, but I need to talk to you in private, so I'm in the bathroom. Nico, I need your help."

Nico swears again. "I'm kind of in the middle of helping your family right now. And I can't believe *I* am the person you're calling for anything. Orlando's right here. He's the one you should talk to."

I know it's only a matter of time before Rome's overbearing nature takes over and he breaks in. He's being patient now, waiting for me on the other side of the bathroom door, but I know that won't last for long.

"Nico, I'm pregnant."

If I thought Nico had reached his max for cussing before, the steady stream of profanity spewing out from him sets me straight. "What is wrong with you? You had one job, Coco! Keep your legs closed. How hard is that? Do you realize the danger you're putting my people in, procreating like this? Who is the father?"

"The baby is Rome's," I tell him, not bothering to ease him into the truth that's been going on behind the scenes. "We've been together—actually together—for a while now. Not just for the cameras, but for real. We didn't think it was possible for him to get me pregnant, but apparently it is. I'm pregnant, and I need your help."

Nico is completely silent now, and for a moment, I wonder if he hung up on me.

"Nico? Are you still there?"

"Tell me you're lying."

"I'm not lying."

"I need you to be lying."

I pinch the bridge of my nose. "Well, I need you to focus. This is the reality of the situation, and I need your help."

I can picture Nico shaking his head. "What possible help do you think I can give you?"

I swallow hard. "I need to be the Last Deadblood. Maybe we could wait it out and see if the baby is a boy, but even so, the world can't handle my blood. You see what it's done to Fintan. He... He murdered my..." My chest starts jumping unevenly as panic begins to set in.

Nico's reply is surprisingly calm—two words that go together when referring to the youngest Valentino. "I know, Coco. We'll find Fintan. He won't get his hands on your blood."

"I can't do this anymore," I whisper, swallowing hard when Rome knocks on the door and calls my name. "I need you to meet me. Bring your gun."

"Colette, what are you talking about? I need to find Fintan."

"I don't care about Fintan. There will just be another to rise up and take his place if my blood is still here—if *I* am still here." I hate the words I am about to say, but I know I cannot keep going like this any longer. "Nico, I need you to kill me."

25

ROME'S DREAMS

Nico's reply to my horrible request comes after several beats of stunned silence. "You want me to kill you?"

"I can't go through with it myself. I just can't. But I know this is the only way to put Mayfield out of its misery."

Nico's voice is quiet now. "You don't know what you're saying."

"It has to be you. You're the only one who can see how bad a thing it is for me to be alive. I know that's why you hate me so much. I know it's because I am a danger to you and your people. The world will always fight over my blood. And if I have this child, they will fight over her blood. It will never end unless I end it."

The only sound is Rome's fist on the door, knocking

above the din of the fan overhead. "Coletta, open this door right now!"

I grip the phone, rushing through my plea. "Please, Nino-bear. Do this one thing for me, and I'll never bother you again. Mayfield can be free without me being this looming threat. Please. Please meet me. Please do this for me."

Rome is louder now, so I know I am out of time.

Nico's voice is gravelly. "Where do you want me to meet you?"

My shoulders release their tension. "Thank you." I give him my location. "Call me when you get here. I'll slip out and meet you in the parking lot."

"This is messed up, Coco."

"This is the only way. You've known it all this time. You kicked me in the head, which could have ended me. You owe me this."

He snorts. "I owe you a bullet in the brain?"

"Yes. I've loved you since we were children, and you've hated me for the past decade. Put that hatred to good use. It's your one shot."

Rome picks open the bathroom door's lock and pushes his way inside, his nostrils flared. "Whatever you're up to, I won't be kept out of it. I've been by your side every second through this whole thing. I don't deserve to be kept out now."

Rome is right, but I'm not about to let him in on my

plan. He wouldn't approve, nor would he allow it to happen. He loves me beyond what he should. One of us has to think clearly.

I can't believe it's me.

I end the call and hand Rome his phone. I curve my arms around his neck, pressing my body to his. I love the way his arms curl around my waist as if there is nothing else he would rather be doing. As if his hands have never known hard work or horror.

"Don't scare me," Rome breathes, his heart jumping. "I'm on the edge of my skin as it is. Whatever you need, I will take care of it. Just don't scare me. Don't lock yourself in a room when I don't know what's going on in your head."

I lean up on my toes to kiss him. I don't expect a romantic moment to spring up, but my kiss softens him.

It dawns on me that I might not have more than a handful more of these kisses left to enjoy. When Nico gets here, that will be that.

"I love you," I whisper to Rome as he kicks the bathroom door shut behind him, backing me toward the shower so we have a modicum of privacy. "I had to take care of something, but it's done now. I'm here."

Rome's lips are firm as his hand cups the back of my head. "Good. I need you here. Talk to me, Coletta. Tell me how to be good to you."

I kiss him again, savoring the flavor of his lips, which

never disappoint. "Be good to Declan. That's how you can be good to me. Take care of him. He's fragile but no one seems to care that he breaks. They don't notice because he keeps on moving, smiling, doing."

"Of course, tré-sur. Your family is my family."

And I truly believe Rome's declaration. I know his heart is broken over the sheriff's death. I know he feels the sting of Fintan's betrayal.

My hand smooths over the side of his face as my eyes sweep shut. "I never thought I would fall in love like this."

"Let me build us a life away from Mayfield," Rome whispers, his words rife with heartbreak. "We'll have a home with enough land where our little guy or girl can explore and play without the world bothering us." He holds one of my hands out to the side and marries his hips to mine, moving our bodies together in a slow rhythm.

Most would never guess that Rome Valentino slow dances to no music behind closed doors, but they don't know him like I do.

I wonder if he'll still find reasons to dance after I am gone.

I hope he does. The world needs the gentle sway of his hips.

"Tell me more about that life." I rest my head to his chest while he slowly turns us to a song only he knows.

"Mm." Rome's chin brushes across the top of my head.

"I feel like we should have a horse. Privileged children have horses, right?"

I snort at his imagination. "Sure."

"Declan will be the pediatrician, so we won't have to worry about anything there. No doctor will try to take our child's blood if the baby is a girl. Declan will see to that." Then Rome's imagination opens up. "I'll have clouds painted on the ceiling of his or her bedroom. Sky's the limit with our baby."

I cannot muster up the courage to break his heart, to tell him that our baby will never see the light of day because this will be my last day. I am determined to spend every minute of it in his arms, listening to his dreams so they keep out my waking nightmares.

"She should learn about our history—the real history, not the one the humans tell where vampires are a horrible people. She'll have private tutors. And as soon as Declan and Lucas have a kid of their own, she'll have a cousin. Or he." Rome reaches between us and rubs his knuckle up and down over my stomach. "Whatever we have, he or she will be the first of its kind. Half-human, half-vampire, all ours."

The sight of Rome in love with this baby expands my heart to the point of breaking. I cannot hold myself together a second longer. A sob rises in my throat as I listen to his dreams for our child, for a world that might accept the three of us. It's a fantasy I wish could be real.

How I want it all to be real.

But it's not.

The world can barely tolerate having me in its orbit. And after Fintan's fiasco, I now know that fate has reached its boiling point.

Still, I remain in Rome's arms while he tries to convince me that the world has room for us all...

...while I wait for Nico to put an end to Rome's beautiful dream.

26

FORGIVE ME

I don't know how far away from Mayfield we are. I've lost track of the hours since I called Nico to come to the hotel so he can help me end my life.

Declan is asleep, thank goodness. I don't have a goodbye in me for him. Still, I try, writing a note on the hotel's stationery. My love sounds quaint and cheesy on a piece of paper, but it's all I can give him. I tell him to take care of Rome and to let Lucas heal him however he can.

Declan can be free of the Kennedys now. I whisper to him as much when I fold the paper and stick it in his back pocket while Lucas and Rome talk about whatever plan they think will end the madness this time.

If Declan is the only one of us who survives this nightmare, then the world will have all the hope it can handle. Declan is the best one of us.

When my phone buzzes, I know it's Nico, given that I

don't recognize the number. I text a quick, "I'll be in the parking lot in a minute," but then quickly realize how problematic that will be. Rome freaked out when I went into the bathroom to make a phone call. Rome is like me; he panics when the people he loves are snatched at. I can't blame him for clinging a little too tight.

But I also can't stay. I'll only be putting him in danger.

I try the obvious route of leaving out the front door, but as soon as I get halfway there, Rome pauses his conversation with Lucas. "Where are you going?"

I offer him what I hope passes for a smile. "Just for a walk. I need to clear my head. Get some fresh air."

Rome stands. "I don't think that's a good idea. We need to stay hidden until Fintan is found. You have a recognizable face, tré-sur. Best not show it off until the fat lady sings."

I fist the handle as I draw in a steadying breath. "I lost my father, Rome. I need some time by myself to process it all."

Rome opens and closes his mouth twice before he backs down. I am grateful his phone buzzes, dividing his focus. "Five minutes, okay?" He points out the window of our second floor room. "Right here, where I can see you." He holds up his hands before he checks his phone. "I know I sound like a prison warden, but this is me protecting you. You'll have to forgive me for being a little nuts. I'll calm down eventually."

I shoot him a wry look. "I hope you enjoyed that lie."

The corner of Rome's mouth twitches. "I did. Thanks for asking."

I cross the room to kiss his lips. "You're forgiven for being overbearing. But I still need five minutes to myself."

Please forgive me for what I am about to do.

I kiss Lucas' cheek and then march out of the hotel room with my head high and my heart in my throat.

I take the stairwell, moving to the back of the parking lot, where Rome won't be able to see me. Hopefully the rest of the world won't get an eyeful of the Last Dead-blood's final moments, either.

I feel as if I am floating outside of my body, walking to my grave in heels.

The familiar black sedan with tinted windows is parked in the furthest spot, inviting me to the doom of my choosing. I should walk, but I run to the car and throw open the passenger door. "Nico, thank you. Thank you. After this one favor, I'll never ask you for another thing."

"No kidding." Nico's face is somber, his angular jaw like his brother's as he keeps his face aimed out the front windshield. He is missing the weathered look to his skin, the calm that can handle anything, and the height that sets Rome apart from the crowd.

I don't think either of us ever wished for a future like this, yet here we are.

But another body in the car draws my gaze to the backseat.

"Don't be mad," Nico says. He actually looks worried at my scandalized gasp.

My mouth falls open in horror. "Orlando? What are you doing here?"

"Trying not to wring your neck. What exactly do you think you're doing? How could you do this to Rome?" Orlando leans forward from his spot in the back. "How could you do this to *me*? Don't you know what it is to be linked? To be connected as we are?" He punches his fist to his barreled chest. "I feel your agony! You drink my blood! When you lose a family member, I lose them, too." His voice lowers, but it is no less forceful. "And when you are pregnant, I am just as much connected to that baby as you are. As Rome is."

I snarl at the both of them. "I very much doubt that our bond allows you to feel the fresh Hell I am living through right now. Nico, you are the biggest rat I have ever met." I hold up a solitary finger. "You had one job. One."

Nico keeps his hands on the steering wheel. "I might hate the sight of you, but I'm not killing off a Valentino. And I am certainly not going to tempt fate by killing off my brother's mate. Or my cousin's."

Orlando growls like a tiger at the notion.

I jab my finger on the side of Nico's seat. "I don't care what either of you say. This is the right move because it is the *only* move. I love Rome. Do you understand me? If I love him, I can't let my blood be used as a weapon that will surely be aimed at him if word gets out that I am pregnant with his baby. I can't let the world fight over my blood a minute more. Don't you see that? As long as my heart beats, I am a danger to him! I am a danger to the both of you." I huff my frustration as I tug at my hair. "And you are the last person I should have to convince of this obvious logic, Nico! You've wanted me dead ever since I came back to Mayfield! This is your golden opportunity to right the wrongs, and you bring in big cousin cop?" I jerk my thumb over my shoulder toward Orlando. "You know this is the only option!"

Nico keeps his eyes from me as if I am the one with a gun and I have it pressed to his head. "I was wrong," Nico ekes out just above a whisper.

I gape at him, and finally an incredulous, joyless chortle comes out of my mouth. "Did you have a stroke? I've never heard you say those words before."

Nico lowers his chin, still gripping the steering wheel. "I was angry at you because of your blood and all that. The world worships you for how deadly you are. It's sick. But after I told Orlando what you wanted me to do, he had a little talk with me on the way here. He's... He's pretty convincing."

Orlando opens his mouth, but I turn around and snap at him before he can work a single word out. "Shut up! I'll deal with you later." I turn back to Nico. "I don't want to hear the sordid details of whatever heart-to-heart the two of you boneheads had on the way over here. The only conversation I want to have is which of the two of you is going to pull the trigger. This ends tonight, right now."

Nico keeps his hands on the wheel as if he means to drive us over an imaginary cliff, even though we are parked behind a row of tall hedges. "Orlando's right. You're the toy the world fights over right now, but if you were gone, they would just find something else—some other way to keep us down, to justify their hate."

I speak through gritted teeth. "That may be true, but right now, I am the toy. I am the weapon. I am the reason your father is dead, Nico."

Nico grinds his teeth. "Listen, Coco. I know you're throwing my own words in my face. I get it. I was an ass. But the truth of it is my father was powerful. They aimed their weapons at him because a vampire rose above his station and wanted more than the paltry nothing society has reserved for us." Finally, Nico turns his head to me, fixing me with those Valentino baby blues. "Those same weapons have been aimed at Rome ever since. He needs you, Coco. I can't take you away from him. Not now that I know the whole story. I didn't know he was in love with you when I hurt you. Plus, you're carrying a Valentino in your belly now. Whatever anger I felt toward you, I can't go there anymore."

He swallows hard, his gaze drifting to my stomach. "That baby might be the only Valentino with a solid chance."

I hate, absolutely hate, that Nico has chosen this moment to grow a heart. The time for him to care was months ago. Years ago.

"This is bullshit," I grumble, realizing that if I am going to cross this final line, I will have to do it myself.

Any Valentino worth his salt has a gun in his glove compartment. I yank it open and fish around for the weapon. The steel is cold when my fingers close around the handle. I allow myself a single steadying breath before I press the barrel to my temple and close my eyes.

Nico shouts, but it's Orlando's arm around my throat that keeps my finger from squeezing the trigger. With his other hand, he jerks the gun from my grip, forcing emotion to press behind my eyes as I slump in the passenger's seat.

Orlando steps out of the car, pocketing the gun. He rarely shows his vulnerable side, but agony rips across his face. Then he turns his back to me, leaning his backside to the car door.

Nico shakes his head, his chin lowered. "You really thought you could get one over on Orlando? The two of you are mated. Plus, it's Orlando." Nico shoots me a look of sheer disappointment. "Come on, Coco. Don't do that to him. Orlando needs you."

I scoff through my grief. "I'm doing this for him. For Rome. For all of you. If I am alive, you're in danger."

Nico's sadness is palpable. "We're always in danger, Coco. There's nothing any of us can do to stop that. There will always be hate. Humans will always fear what they can't control."

Nico's growth would be good if it didn't come at such an inconvenient time.

My reply comes out in a whisper. "Do you think a day goes by that I don't hate myself for getting Daddy Valentino killed?"

Nico's eyes squinch shut. "You're hating the wrong person." He motions to himself. "To be fair, so was I. We should hate the people who stole your blood. The people who took you and beat you to further their agenda of making the world smaller. That's who we should hate. Don't hate the weapon; hate the one who pulls the trigger."

I snort a joyless, airy laugh. "Ironic, considering the arsenal you carry on you at all times."

Nico snorts at my jab. Then his jaw firms. "They'll hate me either way. Might as well go down swinging." He glances at me appraisingly. "I thought we were the same in that way. I guess your little stunt proved me wrong."

"It's more complicated than that."

"No, it's not." Nico fiddles with the controls on the dashboard, turning on my seat warmer to combat the snow outside.

It's probably the most considerate thing he's done for anyone in years.

Nico takes in a long breath through his nose. "Look, I understand that you're tired of fighting. Maybe you get to sit this one out, and I do the fighting for you."

I turn my head away from him, staring into the side mirror to study the nuances of Orlando's solemn profile. "You hate me."

Nico doesn't argue, but lets my words remain in the air a few beats without batting them away. "I need hope. That baby you're carrying? That's nature giving the middle finger to the rest of the world. That baby is creating a way when all the roads forward had been blocked off for us. My frustrations with you are nothing compared to that kind of hope. I barely remember them anymore. I want my niece or nephew to have a better life than I have. I want them to have choices where I didn't." He leans back in his seat, allowing a sliver of optimism to creep into his tone. "I want that baby to have everything I can't. If I have to stand guard to keep the world from tearing you apart so much that you'll put a gun to your head, then here I am."

I cross my arms, probably looking childish in my opposition. "Don't talk to me about your stupid hope. I've had it this entire time, and it landed me exactly here."

Nico reaches across the console, leaving his palm face-up as an invitation for me to take or cast aside. "Maybe here is exactly where you need to be. Let me believe in this baby, Coco. Please. Let me believe when you can't."

I blink at his hand as tears wet my lashes. I don't want to feel my resolve crumbling under the weight of Nico's beautiful words. I don't want to feel anything. "I can't fight this fight anymore," I whisper.

Nico squeezes his fingers into a fist, but there doesn't seem to be any malice in the movement. His eyes close as if his heart has been birthed and then broken in a single day. "Then let me fight it for you. All you have to do is keep your heart beating. I know I don't have the right to ask you for any favors, but that's the only thing I want. Please, Coco-bear."

"You're an ass for using my childhood nickname."

Nico snorts. "I know."

Agony drips down my cheeks now as my chin lowers and my arms band around my midsection. My lower lip quivers, because for the first time, I am without a plan.

I thought I knew the way forward. I thought the only way the world could go on in a semi-healthy manner was if I removed myself from it.

It was the perfect plan.

But now Nico is begging me to give his plan a shot, because there are flaws in mine.

It hurts. Everything hurts. I don't want to feel the devastation of my father's passing. I can't wrap my mind around the grief of Fintan's hardened heart.

Most of me wanted to end my life because that seemed the best thing for the world at large. But a small, broken part wanted to pull that trigger because the pain is too great for me to bear for one more day.

I shriek when the door is ripped open, revealing Rome in his rage-filled glory. His eyes are round and rimmed in red. His fangs are exposed and ready for a fight.

He doesn't yell.

He doesn't say a word.

His hands busy themselves extracting me from the car, patting me down as if I am a criminal, checking me for weapons with which I might harm myself.

When he is satisfied, Rome sinks to his knees before me in the snow, his arms wrapped around my waist as he buries his face in my stomach. His shoulders are trembling as his tears wet my shirt.

I broke his heart. On top of everything else that's gone wrong, I broke Rome's heart that only started beating for me.

Regret washes over my insides when I realize that perhaps my way of dealing with the problem was not the only option. Not that I have another idea for how to save the vampires from being targeted with my blood, but now that I feel the tightness of Rome's grip, it is clear to me that I cannot leave this man to fend off the evils of the world on his own.

But I don't have it in me to fight any longer.

My hand drifts to Rome's hair, tangling in the thick, black tresses.

Orlando moves to stand behind Rome, shielding him while his cousin is on his knees. No one should see the head of the Valentino family so debased. Even though the back lot is deserted, Orlando takes his role seriously, standing across from me and staring me down so there is no mistaking that I will take responsibility for making Rome degrade himself so.

Nico comes out of the car and stands to the side between Orlando and me, shielding his brother just as Orlando is determined to do.

"I'm scared," I admit in a choked whisper.

Orlando nods once. "I know, but you have to trust us. We will take care of this baby. We will keep the both of you safe."

"That's impossible," I counter, though not unkindly. "I don't know how to do this." I touch my stomach without meaning to. "This wasn't supposed to happen."

Orlando is ever unmoving. "Actually, this is the only way something this incredible could ever happen. Trust us, Colette my dove. We can do this."

I don't know that I believe him, but if there is a task Orlando cannot do, I cannot fathom it. If he says he will do something, he has given me every reason to trust that he will make good on his word.

I don't trust the world with something as important as this child. I'm not sure I trust myself.

But it's not just me anymore. I have help, even if the world can't understand it.

And with that help comes hope. Maybe I can't feel it completely. Maybe I can't hold onto it with anything but quaking fingers. But for now, the hint of it will have to be good enough. I believed once that peace was possible. I'm not sure I still believe that, but to take that hope away from the men I love would be a cruelty of which I am not capable.

"Back into the hotel," Orlando rules. "We are going to hide out here until we have a solid plan. But no part of that plan involves a bullet in your brain or holing up here for that baby's entire life."

Nico nods, adding his own two cents. "That's right. The world needs to see that this baby has a right to exist—that *we* have a right to exist. You have to make them see it, Colette. And we can clear the way for you to give them a view of the future."

Orlando nods. "Starting with an announcement to the press."

I shake my head, holding tight to the back of Rome's head. He still hasn't risen from his knees, but seems determined to cling to me to make sure I don't sneak off and do anything I can't take back. "I'm not ready to tell anyone about the baby. It's way too early to go public with that kind of information."

Orlando presses his lips together. "I meant playing the recording of what Fintan did to the press so they can see this thing goes deeper than a family feud. Senator Collins needs to be held to account. He's sat on his throne long enough, and shouldn't be able to access it from jail. It's time to put someone in place who cares about *all* the people, not just the people who are like him."

That familiar weight settles on my shoulders. This isn't a life. It's a life sentence. I will fight this battle until the day I die, and it still won't be enough for my child to be able to actually live without fear of the future.

My mother must have felt this same weight, yet she kept going, even when there was no hope that the world would better itself.

Nico, of all people, seems to understand this. He shakes his head. "No. Orlando, the sheriff just died. Fintan is still on the loose. If we play the recording before Fintan is captured, it will get lost in the headlines. My people are still looking for Fintan. They will find him and bring him in. Then, when Colette is ready, she can play the recording for the press. Arrest Fintan first. Then take down the senator with the recording." He holds my gaze and nods. "When you're ready, which isn't today." Nico lowers his chin. "When my dad died, I drank myself sick for weeks. The problems will still be there when you're ready for them. Take your time. Whatever the pregnant lady equivalent of drinking yourself sick is, do that first." He shrugs. "Maybe you can overdose on milk?"

I snort a laugh, surprised that anything is funny today. I nod, taking Nico's suggestion as gospel. "Yes. That's the plan, Nico."

Nico's shoulders lower, his demeanor softening. "Good. I'm pretty sure I can drink more milk than you, but I'm down for some healthy competition. I want my niece or nephew to come out with fat, rosy cheeks. Milk does that, right?"

Rome leans back to sit on his heels, releasing me so I can turn to Nico, where relief from the pain promises to find me. Of all places, Nico is a safe space for me right now when I am desperate for one. Orlando helps Rome to stand, drawing him into a tight hug while I throw my arms around Nico's shoulders.

"Tell me it gets better," I whisper in Nico's ear. "Tell me this isn't all there is for me."

Nico is a novice at hugging, as all the Valentino men were before I forced the much-needed education on them. But after a few beats, his arms coil around my waist. "It gets loads better, because now you have me."

A mixture of laughing and sobbing bubbles out of me, because I can't decide if that is good news or bad news. My heart swells and buries itself in his shoulder, which is surprisingly sturdy when I am uncertain I can stand against the oncoming storm.

Nico holds me in the parking lot while the world tries to crush us. I grip him tighter, clinging to the promise he whispers in my ear.

"Tomorrow is not lost," Nico assures me. "We just have to make it through today."

So we hold each other—two orphans in a world without room for either of us.

Maybe I don't know what tomorrow holds, or if I can stand against it, but with the Valentino men by my side, I am the only one with the backup needed to drag the world kicking and screaming into a better tomorrow.

Love the book?
Leave a review!

27

THE LAST CITY PREVIEW

Enjoy a Free Preview from *The Last City*, the final
installment in the Last Deadblood series

Voting Rights Rally

I t's odd to have no one's hands on my belly but
my own. For the last eight months, it is a rare
moment when there isn't a man treating my bump as if it's
a crystal ball with mystical answers for the future.

The hallway behind the stage is narrow. Then again,
I'm so big that even grocery store aisles seem narrow these
days. It's been a long pregnancy, though, given that this is

my first one, I'm guessing it's not all that different from the average woman's experience.

Swollen ankles aside, it hasn't been too bad so far. I'm just going to push that whole "giving birth" part of the equation out of my mind for the time being, since I have no idea how I am going to get through that.

A problem for another day.

Definitely not today. I have another month to go, so my little mystery baby is staying put for now.

I rub my hand over my stomach. The yellow silky shirt has just enough stretch to it so I can breathe, pairing well with the light gray slacks. The only issue is that the designer made the top backless, insisting that if my words weren't enough to make people pay attention, my outfit sure would. The yellow material is held together by a lacy string that Rome has had a fun time undoing with one of his deft hands. The back is wide open, giving the world a clear shot of my skin, along with the fact that I am not wearing a bra that can be seen from the back. The stylist that the designer sent over insisted my hair needed to be in an up-do, twisted at the back of my head to draw the eye to my long neckline.

I'm just happy I'm not overheating. This backless shirt idea isn't too bad.

Paulo, one of the security guards assigned by the governor, stands at the left side of the hallway, talking into his comm. "The Deadblood is in position. All clear on this side."

Normally I have Rome with me, along with either Nico or Orlando. After the world caught wind of the horror of Fintan murdering our father and escaping with the help of officers on the force in Mayfield, rulers from all over the world offered their shock and horror, but then quickly followed that up with help.

Paulo and Liesl are gifts from overseas. They report back to their country on the status of my safety. They make sure Fintan and his people cannot get to me. For larger events like these, there is a tightknit crew of security men and women out in the crowd on the other side of this curtain, scouring the throngs for signs of malfeasance.

For signs of Fintan.

I hate that this is what my family has become. My eldest brother and I were never especially close, but I had no idea he was behind the kidnapping when I was fifteen, nor that he had designs to do it again—selling my deadly blood to the highest bidder.

I straighten, rolling my shoulders back. "Not today," I vow to myself. Fintan won't get to me today. It took a few weeks to coax me out of hiding, but here I am, giving speeches and campaigning for a better life for us all.

A better life for my baby.

The father of my child rounds the corner. "Are you

ready?" Rome asks me, walking toward me after he ends his call and tucks his phone away.

He needs his hands free to rub my belly.

Sure enough, one hand moves to the base of my spine while the other migrates to my stomach. He leans down to kiss the bump because, you know, it's been a whole five minutes since he's done that. "I'm right here, little one."

Rome takes the time to kiss me gently, settling my nerves that always bubble up at these kinds of things. I love the way his mouth tastes. He tugs on my lower lip, sucking it slightly before releasing it with a satisfied smile. "Mm. Thanks. I needed that."

There is so much of Rome that I need these days. Even rolling out of our bed is a struggle without help. Of course, the daily dose of his blood keeps the larger aches and pains at bay. The doctor keeps checking me for hypertension, given the stress I am under, but Rome's blood heals the broken parts of me, just like his kisses have healed the busted bits of my heart.

"You remember the drill?" Rome asks me.

"This is my fifth speech this week. I know how it goes. They announce me. I ignore all the questions about the baby. I give my speech, congratulating the world on granting vampires the right to vote."

Rome nods, his hand sliding up my bare skin through the gaping vent in the back of my shirt. "And where will I be?"

"Right beside me, which means life is good."

The corner of his mouth quirks, his full lips reminding me just how striking he is. I love the sharp angle of his jaw, his lean yet muscular build and the way his body curves around mine.

Rome's thumb swipes across my bare skin at the base of my spine. "And where are the emergency exits?"

I point to the two obvious ones and then motion to the less accessible one in back.

"Good. And how quick can I get this outfit off you?"

I kiss him once more. "If all goes well, the second after we lock the door to our bedroom."

"That's what I like to hear." He is wearing his standard Valentino man attire: black fitted trousers, a white dress shirt with the sleeves rolled and a silver belt buckle. All of it pairs nicely with his thick, black hair, which I just cut yesterday.

My lust pauses when I notice hesitation in his expression. "What's wrong?"

"Nothing." When he realizes that answer will not satisfy, his shoulders lower. "Nothing important. Orlando spotted Senator Washburn in the audience. I hate that he's here. He voted against vampires getting voting rights, yet he's here at our victory rally? He wants the photo op, like he's all supportive. Makes me sick." Then he shakes off his foul mood. "I'll get over it. See? Like I said; it's nothing."

"I hope the people see him for what he is."

"They never do."

I run my fingers along the sharp edge of his jaw. I love the way his ice blue eyes are fixed on me. They drink in my form without holding back his affection, which is always married with attraction.

It is a heady thing to be adored by a Valentino man.

When Paulo clears his throat and nods our way, I know that's my cue.

Rome squeezes my hand. "You've got this."

I slip off my flats and toe my feet into the stilettos I know will command the most attention. Even though this is not the time to be testing my balance or my sore ankles and back, it will only be for the twenty minutes or so that I can tolerate the press. Then I will go back to my flats, which are lined with fur and feel like I am walking on clouds.

I roll my shoulders back and don the breezy yet controlled expression which communicates to the world that I am in charge.

My footsteps are sure as I move from behind the curtain, taking the center stage without guessing at my mark. I know the spotlight will follow me. People will listen because I tell them to.

At least, that's what I tell myself.

There are thousands here today in the city's capital. They gape at me with varying degrees of wariness and wonder because I have done the unthinkable.

I am dating the head of the vampires, and by some twist of nature, I am now carrying his baby.

I am followed everywhere I go now, with people taking photographs and breaking out all their old wives' tales, trying to predict the sex of the baby.

I am not ready for that conversation. That giant exclamation point is reserved for family only for now.

I've lost count of how many officials are here, ready to listen to the speech I have memorized in anticipation of the bill going through. This is a celebration of the hard work we have put in over the past several months.

We did it.

The vampires have voting rights now.

But now that I am standing here, staring at the sea of faces who care more about being able to gape at me in person than they do about the people I am here to represent, my mouth is dry and my speech feels paltry.

I have been working on this bill for months, but now that the win has come, I wonder if anyone truly cares about vampires, or if they are more intrigued in the circus aspect of it all.

I have no notes in my hands, and decide on the fly that I don't need the podium, either.

The stage is mine, so I am going to own the entire thing.

"Good morning, and welcome to the era of regret and repentance."

Nope, that wasn't how my speech was supposed to start.

Rome's head snaps in my direction.

Even though my other mate is at the foot of the stage making sure no one gets too close, I can feel Orlando stiffening when I start the speech by going off-book.

My voice carries easily out over the sea of thousands, for which I am grateful. "Today is supposed to be a celebration. We finally pushed through a bill to grant vampires their right to vote. They pay taxes, just like us. They are expected to follow the law, just like us. Yet they have had no say in who represents them. Finally, they have that right, yet as I stand here, there are those in power who are working to cut the legs out from under this progress." I motion to the area where I know one of my most ardent opposers sits. "Senator Washburn, won't you please stand?" I wait for him to take the position of honor before I unleash. "Senator Washburn is working on an addendum right now to limit polling places in vampire territory. He would like there to be one polling station for the entire vampire populace, guaranteeing that not every vampire will be able to vote, simply because there will not be the hours in the day to process them all."

I can tell the audience is confused. They came here for a rally, to show their excitement for the bill that just passed.

To find out that their victory will have red tape and countless stipulations?

This is politics.

I press on, foregoing any semblance of cheer. "What about absentee ballots, you might ask? Well, that would be a welcome alternative, but for the senator's addendum, which would limit vampire absentee ballots to those with a doctor's note. Being that they don't have medical care at the ready, this does away with all absentee voting."

I will not pause for the shouts of "Boo!" that are erupting all around the massive auditorium. They are music to my ears.

"The addendum also requires a valid driver's ID, which, due to overpolicing in the West End of Mayfield, many do not have. So today I want to congratulate those forward thinkers who voted to grant vampires the right to be heard. But I also want to challenge you." I step forward, commanding the spotlight with sheer ferocity. "The fight is far from over. While for most of you who live outside of Mayfield, this is a problem that doesn't affect your everyday life. But for me, it does. I live in Mayfield, and have moved into vampire territory. The father of my child might not be able to vote to make sure the person in charge cares about our baby enough to protect him or her."

My baby kicks, as if on cue.

My hand moves to my stomach. "So while this is

supposed to be a celebration, it is a pause. Today is merely a breath that we grant ourselves before we pick up the baton and resume the fight for equality." I look out over the faces that have gone from celebratory to hardened with purpose.

Good. They will need that determination if the world is going to evolve.

My voice carries while my baby kicks again. "I have one question for all of you: Are you tired of the fight?"

"No!" comes the resounding gong of enthusiastic replies.

It's a beautiful thing, the cries of the impassioned. I can only hope they last long enough to enforce the change we all crave.

"Then show me how you will protect the future. Show me how you will stand up against Senator Washburn and those like him. He is here today to cash in on being seen at this rally, but he votes against equal rights, like so many others! Show me that your minds and your hearts are open to change, and that you are ready to push forth the policies that must come if we are to call ourselves humane. I..."

I open my mouth, but at that exact moment, I feel something I am not supposed to experience for one whole month.

I was told I had a month. I'm not ready for what I am positive is my very first contraction. My belly hardens and the inside quakes like the echoes of something powerful approaching as it awakens.

Panic strikes my features. Before I can voice anything, Rome rushes to my side from where he stood behind me. His arm winds around my hips, bolstering me should I need it.

I don't think he knows my labor might be starting early, but he knows the quaver in my voice, which is all he needs to hear to move quickly.

Still, I continue with my speech as best I can with Rome by my side.

"Maybe you all don't have as much to lose. Maybe it's not your child who will be silenced if this bill is not left unadulterated. But I like to believe that you are the kind of people who care even about children who are not yours, because that's how big your hearts are. You don't care if a person is a vampire or a human, a boy or a girl. You care that there is a chance for kindness in the world." I stand my ground, willing my child to wait just a few more minutes. My eyes glisten with passion that is now mingled with fear.

I was supposed to have more time.

"I trust you all know how to give Senator Washburn a piece of your minds. I trust you know how to vote him out of office for attempting to silence those who deserve to be heard. He would make your protests and votes a struggle for nothing. He would take your voices and silence them if they don't preach the bigotry that got him elected in the first place." I rub my stomach. "My child deserves better, and so do yours."

My child rolls in my stomach like the baby is trying to breakdance.

I gasp, letting my panic broadcast across my face.

I am not sure how long I can keep up the façade of everything being business as usual.

"Now, if you'll excuse me, Governor Ingrid Mason is going to field any of your questions concerning how best to vote Senator Washburn out of office. She can walk you through how you can help those who have been ostracized and belittled under the guise of civilized behavior." I rub my stomach near the bottom of the bump, worried that I somehow need to hold my baby inside of me for just a little while longer, and perhaps I can achieve this feat by pressing my hand to my stomach. "I expect you will have this amendment thoroughly dealt with before my child is born. I also anticipate your passion for justice will rush the necessary changes because I am pregnant, and I can't do this all by myself. I need you to fight this battle for me for just a little while, so I can give birth and start a new lega-cy." Emotions aren't exactly a rare occurrence these days, but it still surprises me when I tear up, especially in public. "I need you to make sure there is room in this world for my child. I believe the world is big enough for us all, but you might have to prove that to yourselves, and to the policy-makers who vote as if it's not."

Rome's hand moves to my stomach, and as if on cue, my belly hardens and quakes again, tightening my insides with pain enough to take my breath away.

Rome's eyes widen as all color drains from his face. "Was that... Are you..."

"Governor Ingrid Mason, everybody." I introduce her to the stage and grip Rome's hand tighter than a lesser man might be able to tolerate. We exit the stage at a leisurely pace.

Because I should have a month.

I'm not ready for this...

...Yet here we go.

Finish the series and read *The Last City* today!

ABOUT THE AUTHOR

USA Today bestselling author Mary E. Twomey lives in Michigan with her three adorable children. She enjoys reading, writing, vegetarian cooking, and telling her children fantastic stories about wombats.

While she loves writing fantasy, dystopian, and paranormal tales for her readers, Mary also writes romance under the name Tuesday Embers, and cozy mysteries under the name Molly Maple.

Visit her online at www.maryetwomey.com, and sign up for her newsletter, so you never miss a new release.